SPRING BREAK

In no time flat, the seat belt sign was on again. Elizabeth had to swallow hard to clear her ears while the plane swooped downward. She noticed Jessica nervously clutching the armrests as the wheels of the plane were lowered and the ground seemed to jump up at them. But as soon as they had touched down smoothly, Jessica was all smiles again.

"Come on, Liz!" Jessica exclaimed. "I want us to be the first ones off this plane!" She was up the second the seat belt sign went off.

"What happened to the Jessica Wakefield who always takes her time?" Elizabeth teased.

"Liz," Jessica responded in dead earnest, "we've only got a week. I don't intend to waste a minute more of it in this airplane."

Jessica was right. This was going to be a vacation they would remember forever. There wasn't a second to lose!

Bantam Books in the Sweet Valley High Series
Ask your bookseller for the books you have missed

#1 DOUBLE LOVE
#2 SECRETS
#3 PLAYING WITH FIRE
#4 POWER PLAY
#5 ALL NIGHT LONG
#6 DANGEROUS LOVE
#7 DEAR SISTER
#8 HEARTBREAKER
#9 RACING HEARTS
#10 WRONG KIND OF GIRL
#11 TOO GOOD TO BE TRUE
#12 WHEN LOVE DIES
#13 KIDNAPPED!
#14 DECEPTIONS
#15 PROMISES
#16 RAGS TO RICHES
#17 LOVE LETTERS
#18 HEAD OVER HEELS
#19 SHOWDOWN
#20 CRASH LANDING!
#21 RUNAWAY
#23 SAY GOODBYE
#24 MEMORIES
#25 NOWHERE TO RUN
#26 HOSTAGE!
#27 LOVESTRUCK
Super Editions: PERFECT SUMMER
                SPECIAL CHRISTMAS
                SPRING BREAK

SWEET VALLEY HIGH
Super Edition

SPRING BREAK

Written by
Kate William

Created by
FRANCINE PASCAL

BANTAM BOOKS
TORONTO · NEW YORK · LONDON · SYDNEY · AUCKLAND

RL 6, IL age 12 and up

SPRING BREAK
A Bantam Book / April 1986

Sweet Valley High is a trademark of Francine Pascal

Conceived by Francine Pascal

Produced by Cloverdale Press, Inc.
133 Fifth Avenue, New York, N.Y. 10003

Cover art by James Mathewuse

ISBN 0-553-25537-1

Published simultaneously in the United States and Canada

PRINTED IN THE UNITED STATES OF AMERICA

O   0 9 8 7 6 5 4 3 2 1

To A. Kane G.

One

Elizabeth Wakefield peered out the narrow airplane window and waved vigorously to the three tiny figures standing by one of the windows of the international departures building.

"Liz, I don't know why you're bothering," her twin sister, Jessica, said, settling into her seat, waiting for the plane to take off. "They can't even see you."

"Oh, Jess, I know. It's really more for myself than for them. I kind of wanted one last good-bye. Know what I mean?" She kept waving at her parents and her brother, Steven.

"No, I don't know what you mean," Jessica answered with a trace of annoyance. "It's only

1

spring vacation. You've been away lots longer than this before."

Elizabeth laughed. "You're right, but somehow this seems like a bigger deal than any of those other times. Jessica, when we wake up tomorrow, California's going to be six thousand miles away! Now don't tell me that you aren't just the teensiest bit nervous about that, Miss Calm, Cool, and Collected." She gave her twin a playful poke in the ribs.

Ms. Dalton, the French teacher at Sweet Valley High School, had arranged an exchange program for this vacation, and now, after much excitement and planning, Elizabeth and Jessica were on their way to Cannes, a glamorous city on the French Riviera.

Jessica tried to look nonchalant, but Elizabeth saw her sit straight up as a young couple sitting across the aisle from the twins began speaking to each other in French. It was impossible not to be excited.

"Liz, listen!" Jessica's forehead wrinkled in concentration as she tried to catch some of the couple's conversation. After a few seconds a scowl appeared on her face. "I know I ought to study a little harder in Ms. Dalton's class, but this is ridiculous! I don't understand a word, do you?"

"Not much," Elizabeth admitted, "but don't worry. You know what Ms. Dalton said. It's going to take us a while to get used to hearing real French. We'll start catching on—"

"When?" Jessica interrupted, her blue-green eyes flashing as she bounced up and down on the blue cloth seat. "We only have a week!"

"Ten days," Elizabeth corrected, "and you just have to stick with it and be patient." But as Elizabeth was well aware, patience was one of the seven deadly sins in Jessica Wakefield's book.

"Well, I've heard that everybody over there speaks English anyway," Jessica replied.

"Honestly, Jess, one of the reasons for taking this trip is to practice our French." Elizabeth sighed. Identical on the outside, from their all-American good looks to their perfect size-six figures and blond, shoulder-length hair, she and her sister were as different on the inside as they could possibly be.

Elizabeth was generous and open, honest and loyal. She believed the best about people. And while Jessica was dazzling, popular, and loads of fun, she was very, very devious. What she wanted, she got, no matter whose toes she had to step on along the way.

Now Jessica addressed her sister as the last few passengers found their seats. "Maybe *you're* going to France to practice your French," she said, "but I'm going to have a good time—and that's all."

"You don't have to make me out to be some

3

kind of boring wimp," Elizabeth protested. "I have every intention of having a fantastic time. It just so happens that I think it'll be incredibly exciting to be speaking a foreign language."

Jessica shrugged. "Maybe for you." She turned away from the French-speaking couple to regard the portly, balding man in a gray pin-striped suit sitting next to her.

She and Elizabeth watched as he tucked a pillow under his head, reached into his attaché case, and pulled out a black satin sleep mask. He strapped it over his eyes and stretched his legs out under the seat in front of him.

"I guess he needs his beauty sleep," Jessica whispered in Elizabeth's ear.

Elizabeth stifled a giggle. "Right. When he wakes up at the end of the trip, he's going to look just like Robert Redford!"

Their laughter was interrupted by the crackle of a loudspeaker. "Good afternoon, ladies and gentlemen," a woman's voice said. "Welcome aboard flight seven-thirty-four. Destination, Nice, France, via Kennedy International Airport in New York City."

Elizabeth gave a shiver of anticipation.

The woman's voice continued to fill the cabin of the plane. "Flight time to New York will be approximately six hours, twenty minutes; and flight time from New York to Cannes will be about seven hours. There will be a forty-five minute stopover at Kennedy while we refuel.

4

Passengers may deplane there for one half hour. We expect to arrive in Nice at twelve forty-five P.M., local time. We ask now that you check to see that your seat belts are fastened, your seats are in the upright position, and that you have extinguished all smoking materials."

The loudspeaker crackled again, and a deeper voice came over. *"Bonjour, mesdames et messieurs,"* it began. *"Bienvenue au vol sept-cent trente-quatre."*

Elizabeth could hardly contain herself. "Jess, we're going! We're really going!" She grabbed Jessica's arm and gave her a squeeze as the rest of the message was repeated for the French-speaking passengers. Even Jessica's mask of disinterest slipped for a moment.

Several flight attendants then took their places at different points in the plane to demonstrate the use of the oxygen masks and explain safety procedures.

Jessica's happy expression vanished. "I hate this part," she grumbled. "It reminds me of all the horrible things that can happen while you're up in the air. Why can't they just leave it out?"

"It's only a precaution, like putting on your seat belt," Elizabeth reassured her twin. Although Jessica would never admit it, Elizabeth knew that flying sometimes put her sister on edge. "Don't worry, Jess."

"I'm not worried," Jessica retorted. "But I

don't want to spend the beginning of my vacation thinking about that kind of stuff."

"Then don't." Elizabeth gave her twin a comforting pat on the knee. "There are plenty of other things to concentrate on. Like the fact that we're moving, for one." She leaned back in her seat so that her sister could have a clear view out the window.

"Hey, you're right! Look. Mom and Dad and Steven are getting farther away!"

Elizabeth glanced back at her family one last time as the plane rolled forward. The flight attendants took their seats, and the airplane's speed increased as it taxied down the runway. The engines roared. The plane's vibrations filled Elizabeth's body as they streaked past the terminal buildings. The nose of the jet pointed upward, and they were off the ground. Elizabeth felt herself being pinned back in her seat by the forward momentum of the craft. They climbed upward. A few minutes later the plane leveled off, and the engines quieted. They were in the air and on their way!

The plane glided along smoothly above a landscape of wispy, cotton-white clouds. Elizabeth studied the letter from the Glizes, the family she and Jessica would be staying with in Cannes. They had enclosed a photo along with it. The mother, Avery Glize, was slender and petite.

6

Her hair was cropped fashionably short, and she was dressed in a navy skirt and soft-looking V-neck sweater. Her son, René, who was almost eighteen, was tall and fair-haired. His tightly fitting jeans were unmistakably French. At one side of the snapshot, her head turned away from the camera, was a girl with wavy red hair, Rene's younger sister, Ferney.

Elizabeth squinted at the photo, trying to get a better look at Ferney. Did she have her brother's large eyes and high cheekbones? Her mother's creamy complexion? Was she, at this same moment, examining the picture the Wakefields had sent her as her own flight carried her toward California for this spring-break exchange?

There was no Monsieur Glize in the picture. Avery Glize had mentioned in the letter that it was just her and her children in their spacious house. There was plenty of room, she had said, so it would be no trouble hosting both the twins in exchange for Ferney's stay in Sweet Valley. Of course Elizabeth and her family had wondered about M. Glize. Where was he?

"Hey, Liz, are you sticking your nose in that letter again?" Jessica was climbing back into her seat after a trip to the rest room, stepping over the heavyset man, who had woken up when lunch was served, only to go right back to sleep as soon as his tray was cleared away. "You're going to miss all the action that way," Jessica continued. "There are some really cute guys on this flight, you know. If you take a walk back to the rest room, check out the one sitting on the right, all the way in the back."

"Actually, I think this one is kind of good-looking." Elizabeth put her index finger on the picture of René. "So French, don't you think?"

"You like him already, don't you?" Jessica asked.

Elizabeth could feel the heat rising to her face. "All I said was that he was attractive," she murmured defensively. "So don't start jumping to any conclusions. I haven't even met the guy."

"But when you do, and he turns out to be nice . . ." Jessica persisted.

"Jess, I know what you're trying to do, and I appreciate it," Elizabeth said, "but you've got to let me take things in my own time, OK?"

"Liz, you've had plenty of time. If you keep this up, you're going to become a number-one candidate for a convent." She shook her head, her blond hair swinging from side to side. "I certainly don't need to remind you that Todd moved to Vermont ages ago."

Elizabeth nodded. "No, you don't."

"So?"

She was cornered by Jessica's penetrating gaze. "So, nothing. The right guy just hasn't come along yet. Todd's a hard act to follow."

Elizabeth pictured her ex-boyfriend's warm brown eyes, his lopsided grin, his lean, muscular basketball player's body. She knew she was no longer in love with him, but she hadn't met anyone she could care about the way she had cared about Todd.

"Well, listen, Liz," Jessica was saying, inspecting the photograph herself, "if you don't want this guy, let me know. He's really not bad." She shook the picture at her sister. "But if you like him . . ."

"We'll see, Jess. I don't think I'm ready for anything too serious yet."

"Then this is perfect! You can't get too serious about someone who lives so far away, plus we're not going to be there for that long anyway. Just what the doctor ordered—a little nice, easygoing vacation fun." Jessica winked. "I intend to have a lot of it."

"I'll think about it, Dr. Wakefield," Elizabeth joked back, "but let's meet the guy first."

"Sure."

Elizabeth let out a tiny sigh of relief. She was off the hook. At least for the moment. "So, how do you think Ferney's going to like staying in Sweet Valley?" she asked, quickly steering the conversation to a safer topic.

"Well, Steve said he'd take her around and introduce her to everyone," Jessica said. "Maybe bring her to the Beach Disco this weekend. You know, last time Lila Fowler came back from France, she told me that the kids over there really like American music."

"Oh, you mean this is going to be Lila's second trip to France?" Elizabeth mused. "I didn't realize that."

"Third," Jessica answered. "She's so lucky. The family she's staying with has an apartment in Paris *and* a house in Normandy. I wonder how much her dear old loaded dad slipped to the French Club so that his precious daughter could be put up in the kind of luxury she's used to." She stuck her bottom lip out. "Some people get all the breaks."

Elizabeth rolled her eyes. "Jessica, first of all, you know as well as anybody that the French Club tried to be as fair as possible when they arranged these exchanges. I don't have to point out that the Glizes agreed to host you and me both, and Lila's family didn't. Second, if you want to talk about 'some people,' some people— like Enid—have to stay in Sweet Valley and baby-sit this vacation to earn a little pocket money. Not everybody is lucky enough to be going on this trip."

Jessica wrinkled her small, perfect nose. "Enid, Enid, Enid. I don't know why you spend so much time with that nerd. She gives me a royal pain in the neck."

"That's beside the point." Elizabeth's voice grew sharp. "But if you insist on pursuing this, Enid Rollins is my best friend. She's smart and fun and sweet—"

"Oh, all right, Liz, I've heard it all before," Jessica cut in.

Elizabeth kept her gaze on her twin.

"Liz, stop looking at me that way. I'm sorry. OK? I apologize."

Elizabeth nodded, and her expression softened. "Anyway, I was just using Enid as an example. Lots of other people had to stay home this vacation, too. Cara, for instance."

Cara Walker was Jessica's best friend and their brother Steven's new girlfriend.

"Yeah, but she and Steve are really happy about getting to spend some time together. God, those two are getting so domestic lately, I can't stand it."

"Jessica Wakefield! You were the one who was always trying to get them together. You should be happy for them."

"I am. It's just that Cara is so— I don't know. . . . She's changed."

"I agree with you there. She's grown up a lot. Enough for Steve to finally become interested in her. Maybe that means she has less time for you, but, Jess, you've got to admit that it's finally good for Steve. It took him so long to get back on his feet after Tricia. . . ." She let her sentence trail off. Even after all these months, it was too painful to say it out loud.

Tricia Martin, beautiful, generous Tricia, had been Steven Wakefield's girlfriend. Her painful death from leukemia had devastated everyone who knew her. Afterward, Elizabeth had feared that Steven would never recover from the shock and grief.

A heavy silence filled the air. Then Elizabeth took a deep breath and squeezed the image of the delicate, strawberry-blond-haired girl out of her mind. It wouldn't do a bit of good to think about Tricia. "So what were we saying?" she wondered aloud.

"Cara," Jessica reminded her.

"Oh, right. Well, I think it's great that Steve's found somebody so special again."

"See? If it can happen to him, it can happen to you," Jessica teased, her tone lighter now.

Elizabeth glanced at the picture that was still in her hand and blushed. "I thought we'd finished with that subject."

"I saw you looking at him, Liz. Don't deny it!"

Elizabeth was sure her face matched the color of the red strap on her new watch. "I was not. I was looking at the house in the background. Did you notice this view?" She pointed to the photograph. Behind a whitewashed stone house were rows of silvery trees stretching across a large orchard that appeared to drop off suddenly. Beyond the rocky cliff could be glimpsed the turquoise waters of the Mediterranean Sea.

"It is pretty amazing," Jessica said. "I guess we *are* lucky, huh?"

"That's what I was trying to tell you. Maybe next time you'll listen to me, little sister." Jessica was the younger of the twins by four minutes, although there were times when it seemed more like four years. Elizabeth gave her a poke in the side.

"Yow! Don't!" Jessica squealed loudly. She reached over and tickled Elizabeth under the arm.

"Jess, please!" Elizabeth's peals of laughter mingled with her twin's.

The man next to them groaned and shifted in his seat. That just made Elizabeth and Jessica laugh harder.

As her giggling fit subsided, Elizabeth leaned over and gave her sister an impulsive hug. "I'm so glad we're doing this together," she said.

Jessica returned the hug. "Me, too. It's going to be the best! The absolute best!"

Two

Elizabeth raced through the passageway from the main terminal at Kennedy International Airport in New York City to the gate where their plane was waiting, Jessica hot at her heels.

"Glad to see you made it back, girls," the head flight attendant said with a smile as they rushed through the door to the plane. "We were afraid we might have to leave without you!"

Elizabeth shook her head at Jessica as they made their way back to their seats. "That's the last time I ever let you loose in the duty-free shop when we've only got a half hour."

"But Liz, it's New York. Some of the greatest things in the world are sold here. You can't really blame me."

Elizabeth shook her head. Jessica would never get over her love of shopping.

The twins edged around the sleeping man and settled back into their seats. "Geez, you'd think he was drugged or something," Elizabeth whispered.

"Nah, he's just the shy type," Jessica said and giggled.

They barely had time to buckle themselves in when the flight attendant's voice came over the loudspeaker to welcome them back aboard and give them flight information again in two languages.

"I'm beginning to feel like a real pro at this," Elizabeth said.

"Yeah, I know what you mean." Jessica didn't seem quite so nervous as they lifted off for a second time.

The sun was setting, and crimson streaks split the purple sky. Below, Elizabeth could see millions of twinkling lights that illuminated the huge city like decorations on a giant forest of Christmas trees. It was spectacular.

The plane continued to soar upward, and soon New York City disappeared as they passed through a thick cloud cover. "Next stop, Nice," Elizabeth whispered.

After the plane leveled off, she took out her diary and tried to write down everything that had happened so far. Elizabeth wrote in her diary every day, in addition to writing articles for the school newspaper and writing short stories and poems, which she was unwilling to show anyone. She loved to write. It helped her feel better when she was sad or confused, and it helped her savor the good moments, also. Her ambition was to someday be a real, published author.

Usually, her thoughts flowed easily, a rushing stream of ink on paper. But now the page remained blank. This was one of those times when Elizabeth was too excited for words.

Eventually she gave up and plugged the extra set of headphones into Jessica's Walkman. The rough, energetic sound of The Droids, Sweet Valley High's favorite student band, filled her ears, and Elizabeth tapped her foot in time to the beat.

After serving drinks, the flight attendants began serving dinner. "What do you think this is supposed to be?" Jessica asked, inspecting the contents of the foil tray in front of her. She took her fork out of its plastic wrapper and pushed around what was apparently the main course.

"Got me," Elizabeth said, unwrapping her meal. "Looks just like what they gave us for lunch."

"Except they're trying to add a continental touch," Jessica noted, prodding the tiny sliver of Brie with the back of her fork. *"Le fromage,"* she enunciated, sounding pleased that, if nothing else, she remembered the French word for cheese.

"That's probably the only edible thing on there," Elizabeth commented. "Let's see what else there is. Hmm. Mystery meat stuffed with airplane glue, a side of soggy green beans, and a piece of cake. Or is that a sponge?"

"Triple yuck," Jessica declared, taking a bite of the cake and throwing the rest back down on her tray. "This is worse than the stuff they serve in the cafeteria."

Elizabeth was relieved when the flight attendants finally collected the trays. Afterward, they brought around headphones for the movie. Elizabeth had seen the movie they were showing twice already, but she and Jessica both decided to make it three times apiece. They settled back in their seats and waited. But even before the credits were finished, Elizabeth's eyelids were drooping shut.

She had thought she was too excited to sleep, but before she knew it, she was waking up. The sun was streaming into the plane, and breakfast was being served. Next to her, Jessica rubbed her eyes and lifted her head.

"What's going on? Didn't we just have dinner?" Jessica asked groggily.

In response, the loudspeaker rumbled. "Ladies and gentlemen, we are now about an hour and fifteen minutes from our destination. After breakfast, we will be coming around with disembarkation cards. Please fill them out and be ready to present them with your passport at customs upon our arrival."

Elizabeth bolted upright. Passports! Customs! When she stepped outside next, she and Jessica would be in a foreign country! Outside the airplane window, the clouds had thinned, and the glinting ocean below had given way to land, a collage of fresh green forests, checkerboard fields, and miniature towns that Elizabeth could barely make out from this great height. Roads and streams ran through the countryside like arteries and veins. Elizabeth was so excited she could feel her heart pounding inside her chest.

Somehow she managed to wash and get through breakfast, although she left the airline's attempt at a croissant on her tray, opting to wait for the real thing. Jessica skipped the meal altogether, spending the better part of twenty minutes fussing with her makeup in the rest room. She confessed to Elizabeth that she had also helped herself to some souvenir soaps with the airline logo on the wrappers.

In no time flat, the seat-belt sign was on again, and Elizabeth had to swallow hard to clear her ears while the plane swooped downward. She noticed Jessica nervously clutching the armrests as the wheels of the plane were lowered and the ground seemed to jump up at them. But as soon as they had touched down smoothly, Jessica was all smiles again.

"Come on, Liz! I want us to be the first ones off this plane!" She was up the second the seat-belt sign went off.

"What happened to the Jessica Wakefield who always takes her time?" Elizabeth teased. "I thought 'let 'em wait' was your motto."

"Liz," Jessica responded in dead earnest, "we've only got a week. I don't intend to waste a minute more of it in this airplane."

"Jess, we have ten days," Elizabeth reminded her for the second time, but Jessica had already grabbed her bag and was halfway up the aisle. Elizabeth gathered her carry-on luggage and followed her twin. Jessica was right. This was going to be a vacation she would remember forever. There wasn't a second to lose.

"Wow! I can't believe we're here!" Elizabeth looked right and left, twisting around and drinking in everything in sight as she and Jessica followed the crowd to the baggage claim area.

In some ways it could have been any other airport—the crowds of rushing people, the stark, modern building, the signs in many languages. But it felt different, foreign. Elizabeth caught sight of a little boy dressed in blue, knee-length shorts, complete with crisp white shirt, suspenders, ankle socks, and navy oxfords. He looked just like one of the pictures of a grade-school boy in her text book for Ms. Dalton's class.

"Look, Jess." Elizabeth pointed him out.

"*You* look, Liz." Jessica was staring across the room at a boy of about their own age, his model-perfect features set off by a healthy-looking suntan. "If they all look like that here, you're going to have to drag me back to California," Jessica murmured.

When a girl in a short skirt with large, brightly colored earrings went over and looped her arm through the boy's, Jessica snapped her fingers in disgust. "Wouldn't you know it."

"Come on, sister, dear. Maybe we'd better concentrate on getting our suitcases right now. There'll be plenty of time for boy-watching once we're settled in." Elizabeth led her twin toward the conveyor belt with the luggage from their flight.

They grabbed their bags and lined up for customs. "*Bonjour*," said the uniformed man behind the counter.

Elizabeth felt a smile stretching across her face. "*Bonjour*," she returned, saying her first word of French in that land. She handed him her passport, and Jessica did the same.

"*Ah, Americaines*," the man observed. "*Votre premier voyage ici?*" He spoke slowly and clearly, making it easy for Elizabeth to understand.

"*Oui, monsieur*." She nodded.

"What did he say?" Jessica hissed.

"He wanted to know if this is our first trip here," Elizabeth explained. "I said yes, sir."

"Well, your part I understood," Jessica said, rolling her eyes. "I'm not *that* bad."

The customs official quickly stamped their passports.

"*Bonnes vacances*," he told them. "Have a good vacation," he added with a thick French accent.

"*Merci*," Elizabeth thanked him.

The twins breezed through a set of heavy metal doors and stepped out into the waiting area of the terminal. A large crowd was gathered there, waiting anxiously for their friends and relatives.

"Do you think we'll recognize them?" Elizabeth asked, scanning the faces.

"Don't worry," Jessica replied. "They'll find us. After all, how many pairs of beautiful blond twins do you see here?" She struck a pose for an imaginary camera.

"Elizabeth! Jessica!" As if on cue, a voice floated through the crowd.

Elizabeth turned. A pretty blond woman was coming toward them. Avery Glize. Next to her was René. The boy was tall and trim and wore a sweater draped over his broad shoulders with casual elegance. One lock of straight blond hair fell across his brow. He was even more handsome than he'd looked in the photograph, but at this moment his small, even features were arranged in a sultry pout. Elizabeth's eyes met his, and his expression seemed to soften. But

22

only for a split second. As if he suddenly rer
bered something, the scowl reappeared.

"Elizabeth? Jessica? I know you're the twins,
but I don't know which is which."

Elizabeth's attention was drawn back to Mme.
Glize, who spoke flawless English, with only the
barest trace of an accent.

"I'm Liz." Elizabeth put her hand out.

Avery Glize took it and drew Elizabeth toward
her, kissing one of her cheeks and then the
other. Then she did the same to Jessica. "European style," she explained. "And this is my son,
René," she said.

When René didn't move, Elizabeth stepped
forward and took his hand. "Nice to meet you."
She smiled.

René drew his hand back sharply as if he were
stung by her touch. *"Bonjour."* There was ice in
his tone. He turned to Jessica and gave a stiff
nod.

Mme. Glize's cheery voice quickly put a check
on the tension. "Did you have a nice flight,
girls?"

"Yes, thank you, Madame Glize," Elizabeth
replied politely. "Except that we almost got left
behind in New York." She told Mme. Glize
about their losing track of the time in the duty-
free shop.

"Well, we're glad you made it," Mme. Glize
said. "You must be exhausted from your flight.
Here, René and I will take your bags. We've got

lunch waiting at home, and then, if you like, you can take a nap this afternoon. I know what jet lag can be like." She reached for Jessica's suitcase and motioned to René to carry Elizabeth's. He took it wordlessly. If Mme. Glize sensed that anything was bothering her son, she didn't let on.

Perhaps, thought Elizabeth, René was simply shy. She hoped that was all. She sneaked a glance at him, but he was staring straight ahead as he walked, his handsome face as impassive as that of a stone statue.

"I know it's going to take me quite a while before I can tell you two apart." Mme. Glize chatted on as they moved through the airline terminal. "I can't get over it. You really are—how do you say it?—cut out of the same mold, I think your expression is."

"Wow, your English is really good," complimented Elizabeth.

"You didn't learn all that in school when you were younger, did you?" Jessica asked. "I mean, I've been taking French for two and a half years, and I can just about say 'yes,' 'no,' 'hello,' and 'goodbye.' "

Mme. Glize laughed. "I'm sure you'll improve tremendously while you're here—Jessica, is it? Thank goodness you're dressed differently," she remarked, taking in Elizabeth's brightly patterned sun dress and Jessica's black miniskirt and tank top. "But in answer to your question, I

24

lived in the States for a number of years. I̶̶̶
no better way to learn a country's language tha̶̶
by living there."

The twins followed their hosts out of the terminal building and into the breezy midday sunshine. The sound of planes overhead was accompanied by the blare of automobile horns and the chatter in French of passersby. Elizabeth looked around her, blinking in the bright light, and laughed delightedly. "We're really here! Jess, look at all these tiny European cars!" A bright red Citroen drove by with the top rolled down, two couples and a dog squeezed inside.

Elizabeth felt as if she were in a movie as she and Jessica climbed into the Glizes' sleek silver Peugeot, then watched the scenery roll by as they headed toward the city of Cannes. The road signs, the architecture of the buildings, and the announcer over the car radio all reminded her that she was in a foreign country.

Mme. Glize pointed out the sights as she drove, taking a route that led to the Croisette, the main strip running along the water. Grand hotels and bustling cafés lined the street; and palm trees, cypress, and bougainvilleas shaded the sidewalks.

"Liz, the Mediterranean!" squealed Jessica, poking her head out the window for a better view of the sparkling sea.

Elizabeth felt heady and dizzy. "Oh, it's beautiful!" she exclaimed.

"That's the Carlton Hotel," Mme. Glize said, as they drove by an elegant white, turn-of-the-century building that commanded the entire Croisette and resembled, to Elizabeth, a gigantic white wedding cake. "Many of the stars of the Cannes film festival stay there. René was able to attend some of the films there this year with a classmate whose mother helps arrange the screenings."

"Really?" Elizabeth turned to René and addressed him in French, slowly and carefully forming her words. She wanted to include him in the discussion; perhaps then he would open up. "That must have been—um—" She tried to remember the word for fun. It was on the tip of her tongue.

"Terrific? Fabulous? Exciting? Yes, it was." René didn't wait for her to finish the sentence, responding instantaneously in effortless English that made her attempt at French seem like a garbled joke. "It was just super, as you Americans always say." Elizabeth had drawn him into the conversation, but his biting tone almost made her wish she hadn't.

Jessica didn't notice, however. "Oh, so you speak English too," she observed happily. "Great! I was kind of worried about having to speak French all the time."

René turned around toward the back of the car, where the twins sat, and Elizabeth saw the disdain coloring his handsome face. "Of course I speak English. What did you think? It's just you Americans who have only one language that you expect everybody else to speak! I can't even keep track of how often I've heard some American tourist go into a store or restaurant and start speaking in English. They can't even take the trouble to learn to say 'please' or 'thank you' in our tongue. You people expect every waiter, store clerk, and train conductor in this country to speak English." René whipped back around, his head set at a defiant angle.

Elizabeth's face burned with the fire of humiliation and anger. She knew it was true that some Americans went abroad without making an attempt to learn a few words of a foreign language, and she wasn't proud of it. But not everyone was that way. She wasn't. She had come prepared to practice the French she had learned and to improve with every day she spent in Cannes. But her very first sentence had been cut short by René's scorn. And now he was lumping her in the same category with all the people who didn't even bother to try. Who did he think he was? Elizabeth found herself thinking that despite his good looks, his rudeness made him about as attractive as an algebra exam.

She wasn't alone in her feelings. Next to her, Jessica's fists were clenched. No one put her down and got away with it for long. Even Mme. Glize arched an eyebrow.

"René, that's enough. *Ça suffit.*" Her voice was soft but firm as she addressed her son in French.

Elizabeth thought she heard her hostess say something about how René's English was a gift from his father. Then she mentioned Ferney, who apparently didn't speak much English; Elizabeth couldn't quite catch why not.

The full implication of Mme. Glize's lecture escaped Elizabeth. What role did René's father play in this? she wondered. But René's reaction was as clear as day. Although his words tumbled out rapidly, garbled with fury and impossible for Elizabeth to make out, his tone said it all. His voice filled the car, echoing turbulently. Two words were repeated over and over, the only ones Elizabeth understood. "*Mon père,*" he kept shouting, bitterness and icy sarcasm lacing the syllables—"*mon père,*" which both twins knew meant "my father."

Elizabeth and Jessica exchanged curious glances. Then there was silence, a stark contrast to René's heated words. When Avery Glize spoke again, her voice was heavy. "Girls, I'm sorry. We didn't mean to welcome you so ungraciously."

Even René seemed a little ashamed of himself and made a stiff apology.

"Please don't worry," Elizabeth said, vowing to ignore René's tantrum. "Everyone has those days." She kept her tone light. She didn't intend for the vacation to begin badly.

"No, that's no excuse." Avery Glize apologized again. "René and I must discuss this in private." She gave her son a look that meant business. Then her voice softened. "But enough of that. There are so many things you girls are going to love in Cannes—that bakery, for instance. It makes the best bread and pastries in town."

Elizabeth looked over and saw an old woman and a young girl emerging from the bakery, each with a long loaf of bread tucked under her arm. It was just what Elizabeth had pictured when she was back in Sweet Valley, daydreaming about her trip. She could almost smell the aroma of freshly baked goods. The uncomfortable moment dissolved, and the excited feeling enveloped her once more. She was in France! And nobody, not even René, was going to spoil it for her.

Three

Jessica rubbed her eyes, threw off the covers, and sat up in bed. The gentle light of dusk filtered into the airy room through the open balcony doors. Darn! It was almost nighttime. Here she was, her first day in a foreign country, and she had spent the better part of it asleep.

She glanced over at Elizabeth's bed. Empty. Why hadn't her twin woken her up? She jumped to her feet, quickly pulling on a pair of velour jogging pants and a loose, man-tailored shirt. There were things to see, places to explore, and most important, people to meet. In particular, cute French boys, she hoped. And she wasn't going to get to know any by spending her vacation lying around in bed, although she had to admit that she'd needed the rest.

The morning had passed in a jet-lagged fog. She barely remembered getting her luggage into the white stone house and unpacking. At lunch, she had almost fallen asleep in her omelette Provençale, light and golden brown, and filled with tender sautéed vegetables, even though it was absolutely delicious, especially after all that airplane food. But most of the conversation had been in French, and though Elizabeth had held up her end pretty well, Jessica hadn't followed more than a sentence or two. That had made it all the more difficult to stay awake. She had happily agreed when Mme. Glize suggested that the twins take an after-lunch nap.

Now, however, she was up and ready to go. "Liz?" she called out.

"On the balcony, Jessica." Her sister's voice floated in from outside.

Jessica stepped through the heavy glass doors. "Why did you let me sleep so long?"

"Jessica, you don't have to sound so accusing. I just got up myself," Elizabeth replied. "Look. Isn't it incredible?" She gestured broadly at the panorama before them.

The house was perched on a lush hilltop dotted with stone houses, their whitewashed façades glowing pink in the twilight. From the balcony the twins could view the sea, sparkling far beneath them.

"Yeah, nice. Real nice. Boy, I wish someone had gotten me up sooner. Hey, what's down there?" Jessica pointed at several rows of lighted docks, lined with one majestic yacht after another.

"The Cannes harbor. Impressed?" Elizabeth grinned.

"Wow!" Jessica grabbed her twin's arm. "Do you think we'll get to know any of the people who own those boats?" She had no trouble picturing herself in her gold lamé bikini, sipping a cocktail on the deck of one of the glittering yachts.

"Knowing you, Jess, it's entirely possible. Probable, in fact."

Jessica gave a whoop of excitement. "This is going to be great. But, listen, what are we standing around for, anyway? I mean, we've already spent the whole day doing nothing."

"Watching the sun set into the Mediterranean isn't exactly something I get to do every day, Jess. I'd kind of like to stay here for a bit. It's so peaceful.

"But you go ahead. Madame Glize—Avery, she asked us to call her—went out to do some errands, but she said we could give ourselves a tour of the house, if we wanted, and make ourselves at home. She seems really nice, doesn't she?"

"Mmm. Her son could take a few lessons from her. So where is Mr. High and Mighty? Did he go out, too?'' Jessica asked, anger welling up as she remembered how René had insulted her on the ride from the airport. "You know, I take back what I said on the plane, Liz. I don't think you should have anything to do with that guy. I'm sure there are plenty of nicer people around here.''

"Maybe he was just in a bad mood or something,'' Elizabeth suggested. "Not that I wasn't expecting a little more from him, but I think we ought to give him another chance before we jump to any conclusions.''

"Isn't that just like you, Liz, always ready to think the best about people. The guy practically came right out and told us that he can't stand Americans, and here you are sticking up for him!''

Elizabeth bit her lip. "Well, if that's the case, we're simply going to have to show him that he's wrong. I can't imagine why he's got such a bad image of us, but I intend to change it.''

"I don't know about you, Liz, but I expect to have better things to do with my time. For starters, I think I'll take a look around the house. You can find out all sorts of things about people by where they live.'' She glanced at the view one last time, her gaze resting for a moment on the boat basin, and then went back inside.

"Jess,'' she heard Elizabeth call, "Avery said to give ourselves a tour. That doesn't mean snooping. Just remember that you're a guest here, OK?''

Jessica didn't bother to answer. Avery Glize wanted them to feel at home, didn't she? And you couldn't really do that unless you knew a little about the people you were staying with. And then, it couldn't hurt to learn something more about René, something that might be useful if she wanted to get back at him for that morning. Jessica smacked her right fist into the palm of her left hand. The boy definitely needed someone to teach him a lesson.

She swept through the guest room, where she and Elizabeth were staying, and down a long hallway. Nothing much to look at there except a funny-looking telephone sitting on a low table. Jessica examined it and found an extra earpiece resting at the back of the phone so that a third party could listen to a conversation. *Good idea*, she thought. *They should take a cue from the French and start making those back in the United States.*

Next she poked her head into a room. It was simply furnished, just a bed with a dark bedspread, a dresser, a wall of bookshelves, and a large stereo system. A pair of boy's slacks had been thrown over the back of the armchair in one corner. Pay dirt! Jessica thought. It was René's room. What better place to start looking around? She let herself in and immediately walked over to his night table, attracted by a Lucite cube displaying photographs. She picked it up.

In the first picture, René sat in a crowded café, flanked by two friends. One of them, grinning broadly for the camera, held a mug of frothy beer. Jessica studied the boy. *Cute. Definitely cute*, she thought. *But forget it. Any friend of Rene's is one creep I don't want to have anything to do with.*

She turned the cube around to see the next picture. René again. He looked so happy and relaxed in his tennis whites, a racket in one hand, that it was hard to believe he was the same boy who had been so sulky earlier. But Jessica wasn't going to let herself be fooled. René had made his feelings about her quite plain. She stuck her tongue out at the picture and went on to another one.

This one showed a younger-looking Avery standing on a beach with a tiny boy and an infant. René and Ferney as babies, Jessica surmised. It should have been a perfectly normal picture—a mother with her two children—but there was something that struck Jessica as not quite right. Then she realized that the image was off balance. She looked more closely, squinting in the waning light. The left edge of the picture was slightly ragged, as if somebody had folded a strip and carefully torn it away.

Jessica flicked on the lamp over René's desk. That was better. Now she could really see what was going on. She noticed an arm coming from the missing left portion of the picture to circle Avery's waist, a man's arm. René's father! It had to be! And René had purposely removed him from the picture. Jessica was getting more and more intrigued about René's father.

She turned the picture cube over. "Oh, my God!" Her voice rang out in the stillness. "Liz! Elizabeth! You've got to come here!" She stuck her head out into the hall and screamed for her sister, her shock echoing in every word. Suddenly the mystery about René's father seemed trivial. This was a much bigger matter. She looked down at the picture again. "Liz! You won't believe this! Quick!"

Elizabeth came running into the room. "What's wrong?" she asked, breathless and anxious.

"Look!" Jessica held out the picture cube. "Avery, René, and Ferney, taken pretty recently, it looks like."

Elizabeth came forward to inspect the picture. A gasp escaped her lips. "Jess, it's incredible! It's impossible!" Elizabeth shook her head back and forth. "She's the spitting image of Tricia Martin!"

Steven Wakefield couldn't get over Ferney's resemblance to Tricia. He sat across from her on the living room couch, an ear-to-ear grin stretched across his face. Ferney returned his smile easily.

Who says you need a common language to get a point across? Steven thought. They were doing fine with only a handful of the most basic words and whatever gestures they could think of. Steven felt as if he and Ferney knew each other already, even though she had just arrived in Sweet Valley the previous evening.

He'd found out, for instance, that she enjoyed tennis, just as he did. She sailed, she rode horses, and her favorite subject in school was science. It had taken awhile to figure that last item out, but when Ferney had drawn a bunch of test tubes and beakers on a piece of paper, Steven had gotten the message. They finally figured out that "science" was spelled the same way in both French and English, but the way Ferney pronounced it made it sound like a completely different word.

It was incredible! Ferney wanted to be a scientist—just as Tricia had. Tricia always used to talk about discovering the perfect way to harness solar energy or finding a cure for cancer and other terminal diseases. In the end, one of those cures might have saved Tricia herself.

As he thought of his old girlfriend, Steven felt a tugging, aching feeling inside. The feeling didn't come as often as it used to anymore. In part, Steven had Cara to thank for that. But there were still times when the hurt seemed to descend on him from out of nowhere, a net of loneliness and despair that caught him unaware. It was so unfair that Tricia had to die at what should have been a time of blossoming and growth.

But with Ferney there, it was almost as if some part of Tricia was still with him. There was no mistaking the striking resemblance between the two of them—the cloud of golden-red hair, the round, china-doll, blue eyes, the small, shapely body. And hadn't Ferney just finished explaining that she liked science? There was something uncanny about all the similarities. But they were nice. Steven felt comfortable with Ferney.

In a funny way it was all right that they couldn't say much to each other. The silence they shared made it easy for Steven to indulge his imagination. Just for a moment, he could let himself believe that he hadn't lost Tricia after all.

Of course he was aware that Ferney and Tricia were two different human beings, but a little bit of pretending couldn't be so bad, he rationalized. After all the pain he had gone through when Tricia had died, he deserved a candy-coated fantasy every once in a while, didn't he?

Besides, on a more realistic note, Steven had been powerfully attracted by his old girlfriend's delicate beauty. Since Ferney was practically her double, it was hard not to feel a little of the same thing.

Then he thought of Cara and experienced a twinge of guilt. But Cara would understand, he told himself. She knew that at least a small part of him would always belong to Tricia. Cara had told him on a number of occasions that one person could never replace another, that she never intended to be a substitute for Tricia. What she and Steven had together was new, different, and separate from Steven's old relationship. She realized that Steven would always have his memories of Tricia. So if he was just a little bit taken by Ferney's resemblance to her, Steven felt sure that Cara wouldn't be too hurt. Anyway, he had promised Elizabeth and Jessica that he'd show Ferney around Sweet Valley. And Steven Wakefield was a man of his word.

"So, do you want to go for a drive or something? I could show you the beach," Steven suggested to Ferney, drinking in her trim figure, swathed in a chic European jumpsuit.

Ferney giggled and shrugged, giving Steven an uncomprehending look.

"Drive. You know, in a car." Steven pantomimed being behind the wheel. "You and me." He pointed. "We can go to the beach." He went through a series of charades—lying in the sun, smoothing on suntan lotion, swimming.

"Ah, yes!" Ferney spoke one of her few dozen or so words in English. "This is good!"

"Terrific!" Steven got across the idea of putting a bathing suit on under her clothes, then went upstairs to get his own swim trunks. After grabbing a few towels out of the linen closet, he met Ferney at the front door.

As he slipped a pair of sunglasses into the

pocket of his jean jacket and checked to make sure he had his car keys, the telephone rang. He took a step toward the kitchen to get the downstairs extension, but after a second ring, he heard his mother pick up the call.

"Ready?" he asked Ferney, holding the door open for her. They were heading for Steve's car, which was parked in the driveway, when Alice Wakefield poked her head out the door.

"Steven? Can you come to the phone? It's Cara."

The slight guilt that had bothered Steven a few minutes earlier was back. But this time it hit him with the force of a surprise football tackle. "Oh, Mom, we were just leaving."

"Well, don't you want me to ask Cara to hold on? I'm sure Ferney wouldn't mind waiting a minute." Steven couldn't help noticing the look of concern on his mother's face. It had been there a lot in the past two days, ever since Ferney had stepped off the plane and Steven's parents had remarked with stunned astonishment at how much she resembled Tricia.

Steven wished his mother and father would quit worrying about him. He didn't intend to let himself get all mopey and miserable again about Tricia. Didn't they understand that he had made his peace with what had happened? He was all right now, couldn't they see that? He simply appreciated Ferney's good looks and company.

That was it. And he wanted to show her a fun time in Sweet Valley.

He brushed aside his guilty feelings. He had nothing to feel bad about. Ferney would only be there for a little over a week, and she needed someone to take her around town. "Mom, can you tell Cara that I'll call her this evening?" Steven asked. He ushered Ferney toward his yellow Volkswagen.

It was his job to be a good host to the Wakefields' guest. He was certain that in France, Ferney's brother was doing the same for Elizabeth and Jessica.

Four

"So much for European hospitality," Jessica grumbled, plucking a blade of grass from the Glizes' lawn. Sure, it was pretty, but she felt as if she were a prisoner in a gilded cage. Here she was, all refreshed and ready to go after a good night's sleep; she'd shaken the jet lag and was full of energy, but she and Elizabeth had spent the last half hour sitting on the grass like lawn ornaments.

"Jess, what do you mean?" asked Elizabeth, stretching out to catch the strong rays of the Mediterranean sun. "Avery's a great hostess. That breakfast was delicious. Especially those pains aux chocolat."

"You mean the rolls with the chocolate in the center? Yeah, they were really good."

"So?" Elizabeth shrugged. "What's the problem?"

Jessica clicked her tongue against the roof of her mouth. "Don't be so dense, Liz. Avery is away today, right?" Avery had explained that she was a private nurse and that although she usually could choose what days she worked she was sometimes called in for emergencies. A woman who had been a patient of hers once before was coming home from the hospital that day and would need private care. Avery had not wanted to turn her down.

"Right." Elizabeth nodded.

"So you and I are left here alone in a place we don't know anything about." Jessica pouted. There were probably all kinds of things going on in Cannes, and she didn't have the first idea about where to start looking.

"I heard Avery asking René to take us around today," Elizabeth said. "He might not be your most favorite person, but I'm sure he knows all the fun places to go."

"Didn't you see him sneak out of here on his scooter right after his mom left?" Jessica asked, her voice angry as she thought about René.

Elizabeth furrowed her brow. "No, I didn't," she said softly. "It must have been when I was in the shower." She was silent for a few seconds.

"Oh, well, I guess he'll be back soon," she concluded weakly.

"Right. And I'm the Queen of England," Jessica intoned sarcastically.

"OK, so I guess we'll have to suntan here this morning," Elizabeth said. "I could think of worse things than lying up here with this three-star view."

"Great. I come all the way from Sweet Valley to do something I could do in my own backyard." Jessica tossed her hair back.

Elizabeth sat up and turned toward her twin. "Jess, we could take a walk around the neighborhood, you know. That's a start if you don't want to relax here. Or even better, we could go for a jog. With these great meals we've been having, I could use some exercise, and that way we'll get a chance to see what's around here, too. OK?"

"Well, what I really wanted to do was to check out some of the local hot spots," Jessica said. "Not that I would know them if I stepped on them," she added with frustration and annoyance. "So I guess I don't have any choice."

"Great. Then it's settled." Elizabeth stood up and brushed some dirt off her shorts. "Let's go get into our jogging things."

"Oh, how about your first idea about a walk? I don't really feel like getting all sweated up."

"Oh, come on, lazybones, it'll be good for you." Elizabeth laughed as she pulled Jessica to her feet.

"Are you implying that I have to work to keep my perfect figure?" Jessica asked, trying to keep a straight face.

"Oh, not you, Jess," Elizabeth tossed back. "But you can't send your dear sister out to jog all by herself, can you? I mean what if I meet some devastatingly handsome French boy on the way and you're not around to save me from him?"

Jessica slung her arm around Elizabeth's shoulder. "Well in that case . . ."

"I thought you'd come around. Come on, I'll race you inside."

"Liz, can't we stop yet?" Jessica panted.

"I thought you wanted to see the neighborhood," Elizabeth said, turning back to look at her.

Jessica quickened her stride and came up alongside her sister. "I have. Houses, houses, and more houses. OK, so some of them are pretty impressive, but Liz, if you've seen one mansion, you've seen them all, you know? Stone and glass can get kind of boring after a while." She put her hand on Elizabeth's shoulder and tried to make her turn back.

"Come on, Jessica, just a half a mile or so more. You won't be sorry."

"Right. I won't be sorry because I don't intend to do it." Jessica took a few more steps, slowed to a walk, and then stopped.

"Co-captain of the Sweet Valley cheerleaders, ace tennis player, and you can't clock more than a dozen blocks? I don't believe it, Jess." Elizabeth jogged in place as she addressed her twin. "You're not tired. You just can't be bothered to exert yourself a little bit."

"So sue me." Jessica shrugged. "Look, you keep going if you want. I'll jog back to the house and meet you there. That's enough for me."

"Well, OK." Elizabeth gave a little wave. "See you soon," she called out.

"Yeah." Jessica began pumping her legs again, but only as long as Elizabeth was in view. Once her sister disappeared over the crest of a hill, Jessica slowed to a leisurely pace. No way was she going to spend her vacation putting herself through some grueling running routine, she reflected. Cheering and tennis were different. So were diving, swimming, and waterskiing. Those sports were fun. She always had a great time doing them. But jogging wasn't any fun until she stopped.

Elizabeth disagreed with her and thought that jogging was a terrific way to be alone with her thoughts, but then Elizabeth actually liked writing English compositions, helping her mother weed the flower garden in front of their house, and a whole list of other things Jessica thought should be made illegal in the state of California.

If she and her sister didn't look like carbon copies of each other, Jessica would have been

47

tempted to think one of them had been mistakenly switched with another baby at the hospital when they were born. Not that her sister wasn't absolutely terrific. Anyone who thought otherwise would have Jessica's fiery wrath to contend with. It was simply that she and her twin were like night and day, wrapped in deceptively identical packages.

Jessica looked busily around her as she thought about Elizabeth. She was taking a slightly different route from the one they'd jogged on the way out. On this street the houses were even more impressive than some of the others they had passed, and on one side, between the houses, Jessica could catch an occasional spectacular glimpse of the bay of Cannes.

One home in particular caught her attention. It was whitewashed stone, like most of the other houses, but it stretched all the way across a lawn so immense, with such perfectly manicured gardens on all sides, that Jessica had to stop and stare.

She started as a car whizzed around a bend in the road, splitting the tranquillity of the morning as it made a sharp turn into the driveway of the huge house and screeched to a stop. The door to the streamlined silver Porsche opened, and a man got out, his back to Jessica. He opened the garage, got back into the Porsche, and drove it inside. Jessica could just make out another car in there also. From what she could see, it looked as though it might be a Rolls-Royce.

Jessica whistled through her teeth. Wow! She heard the car engine being turned off and the door slamming. A moment later, the driver emerged, pulling the garage door closed behind him. Now Jessica got a good look at him. He was a boy of about her own age, very short, with frizzy, dark hair, a broad mouth and a long, sharp nose. Kind of funny looking, Jessica thought, but with a setup like this, maybe he was worth getting to know.

She caught his eye and waved. He came closer and smiled shyly.

"Bonjour!" Jessica called out. *"Il fait beau aujourd'hui, non?"* Thank goodness she had at least learned how to talk about the weather in Ms. Dalton's class. She was pleased with herself for being able to comment on what a nice day it was. Maybe there was some truth in what Elizabeth had said during the plane ride. Speaking French could be kind of fun.

"Oui, très beau." The boy's voice was soft and gentle, and as he stopped in front of Jessica, she thought she detected a blush on his cheeks. *"Combien de kilomètres avez-vous fait?"*

"Huh?" Jessica tried to figure out what the boy was saying.

"I ask how many kilometers you run?" he translated slowly, his accent thick. He gestured at her pale-blue jogging outfit and running shoes.

"Oh. I'm not really sure. We don't measure things that way," Jessica answered, flashing her most irresistible, sparkling smile. "How'd you know I spoke English?"

"It is the accent," the boy explained. "You are from the States, no? You look American—tall and blond, and . . ." His voice trailed off with embarrassment, and he stared down at his shoes.

"Well, you're right. I'm from California." Jessica was going to have to be extra dazzling to get this timid young man to open up. Not that she doubted herself for a moment. These sweet, quiet types were a snap to wrap around her finger. "My name's Jessica Wakefield. I'm staying with the Glizes." She extended her hand.

The boy took it. "Marc Marcheiller. It is my pleasure to meet you."

Jessica held Marc's hand a second longer than necessary, until a nervous grin spread over his face. "You're the first person I've met here. Besides Avery and René, I mean."

"Ah, yes. They are very nice, the Glizes."

"Well, at least Avery is." Jessica allowed herself a small scowl at her unspoken implication.

"René, also, I think. You just must know René first," Marc said. "I don't know him so well, but he appears to be a good person."

"Well, maybe." Jessica wasn't going to get anywhere arguing about that jerk René. "But I'm happy to meet someone else my own age. It's my first time in Cannes, and I'd like to make some friends."

"I am certain that will be very easy for you." Marc nodded vigorously. "So—" He paused, and Jessica encouraged him with another smile. "You like Cannes so far?" he asked.

This was just the line Jessica was waiting for. "It seems very pretty," she answered, "but I haven't seen much of it yet. I guess I need someone to show me around. I hear the beaches are terrific."

"Yes." Marc glanced behind him at the bay. "My family is part of a very special beach club."

I'll bet, thought Jessica, glancing again at the exquisite house Marc lived in.

"If you wish, I could—how you say it—accompany you there," Marc suggested timidly. "It would make me very happy."

This was too easy, Jessica thought smugly. "Oh, Marc, do you mean it? I'd love that," she gushed. With this house and those cars parked in the garage, she was positive that Marc's family belonged to the most exclusive beach club in Cannes. What better place to meet the kind of people she wanted to get to know? This was going to be some vacation! Lila Fowler was going to be green with envy when she heard about it. "That would be great!"

Marc's face lit up with delight. "Is this afternoon too soon?"

"Not at all. In fact, this morning would be even better. Listen, how about if I go home and change, and I'll meet you back here in, say, an hour?"

Marc looked delighted. "That is perfect," he managed.

"All right, then. *A bientôt*," Jessica said, telling him she'd see him soon. *Good work*, she congratulated herself as she jogged off, putting on a show of extra speed for Marc's benefit. That beach club was going to be the key to her vacation in Cannes!

"You've met Mr. Right already?" Elizabeth couldn't believe her ears. "I mean, I always knew you moved fast, but this is ridiculous!" She shot her twin a look of amazement as she stretched her muscles out on the Glizes' plush lawn after her jog.

"We-e-ell," Jessica began, "he's not *exactly* Mr. Right, but he seems like the kind of guy who might be able to introduce me to someone who is, if you know what I mean."

Elizabeth arched an eyebrow. "I'm not entirely certain I do. Would you care to explain it to me?" She had a funny feeling that she wasn't going to like Jessica's answer.

"To begin with, he lives in the most incredible, gigantic house. As big as Lila Fowler's or Bruce Patman's. Plus he drives a silver Porsche, and his parents have a Rolls."

Elizabeth sighed loudly and rolled her blue-green eyes skyward. When was her twin going to learn that there were more important things in life than money?

"Liz, you don't have to give me that 'oh, Jessica,' look. It's not just that he's fantastically wealthy. Marc's a really sweet guy, too. He's taking me to his beach club today, and I'm sure we'll have a fun time."

"Well, that sounds great. So tell me, what is it, then, about this guy that doesn't make him the one you want to be with this vacation? No, wait, *don't* tell me. He's rich, and he's nice. I guess that means he's not gorgeous enough to meet Jessica Wakefield's impeccable standards, right?" Elizabeth felt herself growing irritated at her sister. They had had this discussion too many times before. She'd lost track of how often she had tried to make Jessica see how unfair it was to judge boys so superficially, to use them and then throw them away.

"Liz, to say this guy's not gorgeous is kind of an understatement. To tell the truth he's, well—to begin with, he's a good three inches shorter than I am."

"Big deal. Jessica, where is it written that the boy has to be taller than the girl? I don't know what century *you're* living in." Elizabeth stood up, took hold of one ankle, and tugged gently on her leg to stretch out the front of her thigh.

"Liz, that's not the only thing. I mean I've

gone out with short guys before. Chuck Wollman. Remember him? He was tiny," Jessica said defensively. "It's that, well, Marc is, um—oh, never mind." Jessica flung her hands up in the air crossly. "I don't see why I should have to explain myself to *you*. When have you ever dated somebody who was really funny looking?" In a complete about-face, Jessica assumed the offensive.

"It's not like I've dated very many guys the way you have," Elizabeth began. "There have only been a few besides Todd—"

"—who wasn't exactly the worst to look at," Jessica finished, pushing her attack. "See, you're guilty of the same thing you're accusing me of."

Elizabeth shook her head. "Jess, I can't figure out how you always manage to get the conversation so twisted around that I don't even know what I'm trying to say anymore."

"Talent, Liz, special talent." Jessica flashed Elizabeth a toothy grin.

Elizabeth burst out laughing. "All right, Jess. I guess you managed to avoid your daily lecture again. Just do me one favor, OK?"

"Anything for my darling twin," Jessica replied. "Just name it."

"Try to be nice to this guy Marc."

"For your information, Liz, I've made Marc a very happy boy already. You should have seen the look on his face when I agreed to go to the beach with him today. This is probably the most exciting thing that's happened to him all year."

"Jessica, your modesty astounds me."

"Yes, of course. Another one of my wonderful characteristics. And now, Liz, if you'll excuse me, I'm going to go get ready." Jessica was halfway across the lawn before Elizabeth could say another word.

She came back down about fifteen minutes later, her tiny nothing of a gold lamé string bikini visible under her semitransparent cover-up.

"So, wish me luck," Jessica said. "Oh, and Liz? Don't sit around here all day. You really should get out and meet some people."

"How nice of you to be so concerned about me, Jessica."

If Jessica picked up on Elizabeth's sarcasm, she didn't let on. "Well, it's only natural for me to be concerned, Liz. I mean you're my favorite sister in the whole world."

Elizabeth didn't bother to remind her that she was also her only sister. She knew that deep down Jessica really did want the best for her. "Thanks, Jess. Hope you have a good time."

"Oh, I intend to."

Elizabeth watched her twin glide across the lawn, her blond hair shining in the sun as it swirled around her shoulders, her trim, curvaceous body moving gracefully. Poor Marc. He wasn't going to know what hit him.

Five

Elizabeth thumbed through a book about Cannes that she had found on the Glizes' bookshelf, then scribbled notes on a pad. "Boulevard de la Croisette," she wrote. "The Mont Chevalier Tower, the Castre Museum." Jessica was right. She did have to get out of the house. And if René was going to be so resistant to giving her a tour of the city, she was going to have to show herself around.

She looked over her list of places to visit and added one more. She capitalized the words: THE BEACH. She had heard so much about the Mediterranean coast, she couldn't wait to see it close up.

As she folded her list and returned the book to

the shelf, she heard the front door open. Loud voices floated into the living room.

"I asked you to take the girls around today, and now I find out you spent the morning with Edouard," Avery was saying in rapid, angry French. "I'm warning you, René—"

"It's not my fault," Elizabeth thought she heard him say. "You know how I feel about Americans, but you had to invite those girls over here anyway. I don't know what you thought you'd prove."

"René, don't be so rude to your mother. I intended to show you how wrong you are. People are people. They've all got their good qualities and their bad, regardless of where they come from."

"But some people are more selfish than others," René countered. "Some people don't care about anyone but themselves."

"That's true." Avery's throaty voice was tight. "For example, you don't care that you've left your guests totally on their own—"

"Just like he left us," René interrupted.

Elizabeth could hear the icicles of hostility and resentment in René's tone. Who was "he"? Was René talking about his father? If so, what did that have to do with Jessica and her? Elizabeth's head swam with confusion. Perhaps she was misunderstanding what René and his mother were saying. The words were fast and clipped, and there were more than a few that Elizabeth didn't recognize.

"René, I insist that you give Elizabeth and Jessica a chance. You are going to take those girls on a tour of Cannes, and you're going to do it this afternoon. Do you understand?"

"I understand that I don't have any choice."

"And, René, try to be gracious about it. You wouldn't want Ferney to be getting the kind of treatment from the Wakefields that you've been giving the twins."

At the mention of Ferney's name, Elizabeth's glance went immediately to another photo of the girl, which was propped on one of the bookshelves. What *was* her family's reaction to the visitor who looked so eerily like the girl her brother had lost?

"Ned, have you noticed how he can't take his eyes off her?" Alice and Ned Wakefield sat at their kitchen table, the brunch dishes still in front of them.

"How could I not notice? He's been following her around like a faithful puppy dog ever since she set foot in this house." Ned Wakefield shook his head. "They can barely talk to each other, and yet . . ." His sentence trailed off.

"Ferney seems to like the attention, doesn't she?" Alice Wakefield remarked. "She's so flirtatious when he's around—laughing and flashing him looks out of the corner of those big eyes."

"Yes. There's something about her that reminds me a bit of Jessica," Ned Wakefield replied.

"But all Steven can see when he looks at her is Tricia Martin," Alice Wakefield said gloomily. She rested her chin in her hands. Fair-haired and youthful, it was easy to see that the twins got their good looks from her, while Steven was tall and dark like his father. Alice Wakefield's pretty face was lined with worry. "The other day he was so excited because he found out that Ferney likes science. If you ask me, our son's looking for excuses to draw parallels."

"It's hard to blame him. The physical resemblance is astonishing. I have to keep reminding *myself* who she is. Poor Steve must be overwhelmed. I think this could be very dangerous for him."

Alice Wakefield nodded soberly. "It's such a shame. The exchange seemed like such a wonderful idea. Now I'm beginning to feel thankful that it will all be over next week."

"Alice, I'm afraid that it *won't* be over when Ferney goes home. All the memories of Tricia that must be surfacing for Steve are bound to open the old wounds. It could be like losing her all over again. Just when he's gotten back on his feet."

"I see what you mean. And it's not just Steve

who's going to be hurting, either. Can you imagine how poor Cara must feel right now? Steve's been avoiding her. You know, I think the two of them were beginning to discover something very special in each other. She's been an important part of his healing process." Alice Wakefield sighed. "I can't bear to think what might happen if he loses her over this. She must know something's going on."

Ned Wakefield took a swallow of lukewarm coffee. "Do you think one of us should have a chat with Steve?"

Alice Wakefield shook her head sadly. "Yesterday I suggested that he return Cara's phone calls. He nearly took my head off. I don't think he'd listen if we tried to talk to him. It might only make him more stubborn about staying by Ferney's side."

"That girl is *not* Tricia Martin. Steven has to realize it."

"But how do we get the point across?" Alice Wakefield frowned. "Steven insists that the past is behind him and that he's just showing Ferney a good time in the United States."

"It's got to be nearly impossible for him to see the situation clearly. His head must start swimming every time he catches sight of Ferney."

Alice Wakefield pounded her fist on the table. "Ned, I feel so helpless." Her voice cracked.

"Alice, I wish I could tell you everything was

going to be all right. I wish I could tell myself that." Ned Wakefield reached across the table and took his wife's hand. "But I'm afraid all we can do is wait this thing out and be here for Steven if he decides he's ready to talk."

"You're right, Ned." Alice Wakefield stacked some of the dishes and carried them toward the sink. "Well, if there's one consolation in this whole mess, it's the girls' trip to France. Do you think they're enjoying their stay?"

Ned Wakefield cleared the coffee pot and mugs from the table. "That's the one thing you needn't worry about. I'm sure Elizabeth and Jessica are having a fabulous time."

There was no doubt that this was going to be the shortest tour on record. René zipped through Cannes in his mother's car as fast as he could, Elizabeth hanging on to the edge of her seat.

Elizabeth had told Avery that she would be perfectly happy showing herself around if somebody explained how she could get where she wished to go. She didn't want to cause any more trouble between René and his mother than she already had. And besides, she'd thought to herself, she'd probably be better off with no tour guide at all than with one who disliked her so much.

But Avery had insisted that her son take

Elizabeth out. "It's lovely that Jessica has found a friend already, but you shouldn't have to be on your own in a new place. I'd love to show you the sights myself, but unfortunately I have to go right back to work this afternoon. Anyway, René knows more about where the young people spend their time in Cannes than I do. Don't you, *chéri*?"

"Sure."

"Good. It's settled," Avery had said. "I'll take the moped to work, and you two can have the car. René, you'll introduce Elizabeth to some of your friends?" It was more of an order than a question.

"Yes, we'll probably stop by the Festival Café later. Georges and Edouard said they'd be going there." René had been cool yet polite. But the minute his mother had left for work, his attitude changed.

"I guess we're stuck with each other for the afternoon," he'd said coldly. "Just the two of us, since your sister's run off with Marc."

René had quickly left the house, Elizabeth racing to keep up with him. "Here." He had unlocked her door and gone around to let himself in the other side.

Elizabeth had climbed in, staring out the window as René started the motor. Then a peculiar thing had happened. As René reached for the gearshift, his hand had accidentally brushed against hers. She'd turned to look at him. His gaze was on her face, and he seemed to be leaning toward her. She could smell his spicy aftershave lotion, and he was so near, she could have reached out and pushed the lock of fine blond hair back from his deep-set eyes. Was it Elizabeth's imagination, or did an electric tingle pass between them?

Suddenly René had given his head a hard shake. He sat straight up, his body tense. The sensation Elizabeth had experienced was gone—a quicksilver flash so brief, she was inclined to think she had imagined it. René had revved the engine and taken off abruptly with a deafening roar, burning rubber as he peeled out of the driveway.

He hadn't slowed down since, racing down one street and up the next, occasionally pointing to a building or a park and saying something that was swallowed up by the sound of the radio, which he'd turned up to full volume.

René made a sharp turn onto a wide boulevard that Elizabeth recognized both from the drive from the airport and the book she had looked through at the Glizes'. This was the Croisette, the main strip that was the heart and soul of Cannes. On one side, the sea sparkled, aqua and inviting; on the other, hotels and restaurants, cafés and stores beckoned to vacationers looking for an atmosphere of cosmopolitan sophistication.

It was truly magnificent. Elizabeth wished she

could get out of the car and take a closer look. "René, what's going on there, where all those people are standing?" she shouted above the deafening music.

René squealed to a halt. "That's the Palais des Festivals, where the Cannes film festival used to be held. Can't you tell from the way all those American tourists are standing around, staring?"

Elizabeth let his biting remark slide. "Well, thanks for stopping to let me see it."

"We were stopping anyway," René said curtly.

"We were? Oh, are we going to the beach?" Elizabeth asked enthusiastically. "I put my suit on under my clothes, just in case." She looked out his window, toward the crest of white sand. Red umbrellas dotted one section of the beach, blue another, green farther down the coast, and yellow still farther. The book Elizabeth had read explained that each beach club had its own color. Beyond the chairs and umbrellas, the bay gave way to an endless sea. "I can't wait to take a swim!" Elizabeth could almost taste the salt-water on her lips.

"Well, you're going to have to. I have no intention of taking you to the beach."

"You don't?" Elizabeth said, disappointed.

"No, I hate the beach." René found a spot and parked.

"Why?" The beach was one of Elizabeth's

favorite places. As far as she was concerned, there was no better spot to read or relax by oneself or to spend the afternoon with friends, tossing a Frisbee or playing volleyball, swimming and sunning and feeling alive. How could anyone not love it? "René, you have some of the most beautiful beaches in the world right in your backyard, and the water's supposed to be a perfect temperature—"

"I never swim." René cut her off in midsentence as they climbed out of the car. "At least not anymore," he added, his voice softer. He stared out at the turquoise horizon, and his eyes clouded over. "I used to, once upon a time, but then— Oh, what do you care anyway?" His tone became hard again.

"I do care," Elizabeth said simply.

René turned to look at her, his eyes probing hers. For an instant the electric feeling returned. But it was gone a moment later. "Look, Liz, forget I said anything, OK? We don't have all day to stand here talking," René snapped. "I told my friends we'd meet them across the street at that café." He started walking, never looking back to see if Elizabeth was behind him.

She followed along, dodging people strolling on the wide boulevard. René was strange, she reflected. There were isolated moments when he seemed human, almost fragile, and Elizabeth wanted to reach out to him. But as soon as she did, he pulled back behind a cover of nastiness.

Was he playing some sort of warped game with her? Did it amuse him to play with her emotions?

Anger boiled up inside her as she hurried after René. What could he have against someone he didn't even know? Her thoughts returned to the argument she'd overheard earlier between him and his mother. When René talked about the person who had left him, was it his father? What possible link could there be between him and the twins? And how did that fit in with René's hatred of Americans?

In an explosive spark of insight, it hit her. Hadn't Avery said she'd lived in the United States at one point? She'd also said that René's English was a gift from his father. What if his father was American? That had to be it! And he had left his family, probably when Ferney was a baby since she had never learned to speak English. Now it all made so much sense. No wonder René felt the way he did about Americans.

But what about this new piece of the puzzle—René's dislike for the beach? Did that have something to do with his father, too? Perhaps she was reading too much into this, Elizabeth thought. Sometimes her writer's imagination did get the better of her. For that matter, maybe her whole theory about René's father was wrong.

Elizabeth followed René to a table in front of the bustling café across from the Palais des Festivals. She wanted to ask him whether she was right, but she couldn't. He would think she was meddling, and she would only deepen his prejudice about Americans.

Nevertheless, she found herself feeling more sympathetic toward her host. If what she suspected was true, René was probably going through a rough time, having her and Jessica in his home. Elizabeth resolved to be more understanding with him.

Her resolution didn't last long, though. René introduced her to his two friends, who were already at the table, and then proceeded to do everything he could to make her feel left out.

Georges and Edouard seemed like nice people. Georges ordered a coffee with milk for Elizabeth, and Edouard explained a little about café life to her. "Buying a drink's just an excuse to sit here and spend time with your friends, watch people, or read the newspaper. You're really renting the table, you know?" He smiled warmly.

But every time one of his friends began talking to Elizabeth, René changed the subject, jabbering in such rapid French, intentionally loaded with slang that Elizabeth had never heard before, that she was lost.

So much for her patience with René. No matter where his problems with Americans stemmed from, he had no right to treat her this way. No right at all. Elizabeth sighed as she stirred a lump of sugar into her second cup of coffee. If she was going to have any fun in Cannes at all, she was going to have to follow Jessica's lead and make some friends on her own.

Six

Elizabeth walked down the driveway, turned right, and walked up the narrow road to the crest of the hill. She wasn't going anywhere in particular. She just wanted to get out of the house and as far from René as possible. After their miserable day together, she wanted to put some distance between them. Neither Jessica nor Avery was back yet, and she refused to stay in the house alone with that boy.

She had tried her hardest to be open with him, but the more she'd tried, the more René had managed to ridicule her. When she had attempted to participate in the discussion that he, Georges, and Edouard were having about the recent international tennis matches, René had launched into a loud, humiliating imitation of her French accent.

"Come on, René. She speaks very well," Edouard had defended her. "I couldn't do nearly as well in English."

"Well, at least you're sensible enough not to try. But I guess some people like making fools of themselves," René had commented nastily.

When René excused himself to use the bathroom, Edouard had patted Elizabeth on the arm. "Don't pay any attention to him," he said in slow, clear French. "You're doing just fine."

"Yes, you are," Georges had agreed. "I don't know what's gotten into René. He's usually such a great guy."

"I guess he doesn't think much of Americans," Elizabeth had murmured.

"Well, you do know about his father, don't you?" Edouard had asked. "Not that it excuses his rudeness."

"So his father *was* American! I was wondering about that. But isn't Glize a French name?"

"That's René's mother's maiden name. She couldn't keep the name of someone who'd left her stranded like that."

"His father left the family when René was small?" Elizabeth had voiced what she'd suspected.

Edouard had nodded. "I think it was a pretty ugly business. Madame Glize was very young, and she had two little children to take care of.

René doesn't talk about it much, but I guess he's got a lot of resentment stored inside him."

"And now he has someone to take it out on," Elizabeth had remarked gloomily. "I feel sorry for him, but—" She'd stopped short as she saw René returning to the table.

"Feel sorry for whom? Who is our little American friend gracing with so much compassion?" René had uttered, laying on the sarcasm.

Elizabeth had said nothing, hoping René would ease up on her if she showed no reaction to his taunting. But he continued to poke fun at her at every opportunity.

Later in the afternoon, he and his two friends had taken her to a marvelous bistro for a late lunch. At least it would have been marvelous if René hadn't decided to publicly humiliate her.

"Waiter! Oh, waiter, some ketchup, please," he'd called out after the food had been brought to the table. "We've got an American here. You know how they like to drown everything they eat in the stuff. I guess it's because their own food is so bad, they'd rather not taste it."

This had proved too much, even for Edouard and Georges.

"René, cut it out!" Georges had said.

"Oh, you've decided to teach me how to behave?" René had put down his fork and addressed his friend angrily.

"It seems like someone has to," Edouard had added softly.

"You too?" René's venomous tone had attracted the stares of other diners.

The tension at the table was high, and it had only gotten worse as the meal continued. The lunch party had broken up as soon as the last bite was gone. René was barely on speaking terms with his two friends. As he and Elizabeth walked back to where the car was parked, René made it clear that he blamed Elizabeth for that.

"Those two will stick up for anyone with a pretty face. They won't even bother to find out what you're like first."

"And you *have* bothered to find out. Is that what you're saying?" Hurt had colored Elizabeth's words.

René's silence had surprised her. He didn't seem to have an answer to that question. It was as if he'd recognized the truth in her words. And although he didn't apologize for his behavior, at least he hadn't made any more unfair remarks about her on the ride back to the house.

Elizabeth didn't plan to give him further opportunities to insult her, either. As soon as they'd arrived at the house, she had gone upstairs, grabbed her diary and a pen, and set off on a walk.

Now she surveyed the countryside from her hilltop vantage point. Down the road and to the right was an olive orchard. Rows of silver-barked trees were terraced along the mountainside, with low stone walls separating one level from the next. Sunlight gleamed on the spindly branches and spilled onto the ground between the trees.

Elizabeth followed the road to the beginning of the orchard and walked down several levels of terraced earth, until she found a soft, sun-dappled patch of grass. She sat down and let out a deep breath, feeling the tensions of the day draining from her body. The late afternoon air was warm, with a light breeze. She uncapped her pen and began writing.

She described everything about their vacation thus far—their flight, the house they were staying in, the city of Cannes, Avery—every-thing except Rene. He didn't deserve one word, she decided.

When she finished making her diary entry, Elizabeth closed the navy, cloth-bound book, stretched out on the sweet-smelling ground, and closed her eyes. Birds chirped, and farther off she could hear the sounds of children playing. She could feel herself drifting off into sleep, images of home mixing with the sensations of the waning afternoon.

Suddenly something wet trailed across her face. Her eyes flew open, and she jolted upright. When she saw the adorable German shepherd puppy, his moist, pink tongue lolling out the side of his mouth, she laughed out loud. "Well, hello there. Trying to scare me, huh?"

The puppy wagged his tail and bounded

toward Elizabeth again, nuzzling her and licking her cheeks.

"Whoa! Whoa, boy!" Elizabeth giggled, putting an arm around the puppy's middle and stroking his back. The puppy calmed down and lay down next to her, his soft, innocent face in her lap.

When Elizabeth reluctantly rose to go a few minutes later, the puppy began following her. "I like you too, boy, but you have to go home," she said, petting the dog. "Is that home?" She pointed to the house on a crest above the orchard. "Go home, boy!"

But the puppy continued to trot along at her heels. Elizabeth sped up, hoping he would go back where he belonged, but he kept up with her. She stopped, and he stopped too, looking up at her with a curious expression.

Elizabeth knelt down. "I don't want to get you lost, see?" She scratched the underside of his neck. Her fingers brushed against a metal tag dangling from his collar. She inspected it carefully. Nykki, it read. Villa de Willenich.

"Nykki," Elizabeth said. The puppy's tail went back and forth as he recognized his name. "Well, I guess we're going to have to find out where Villa de Willenich is and take you back to your owner. I'd be missing you if you were mine." She patted Nykki's head. "Come on, boy!"

She climbed back up to the road, Nykki

bounding along by her side. As she turned back onto the main road, she passed a sprawling home with two little boys playing in front. "Nykki!" one of them shouted, running up and throwing his arms around the dog.

"*Bonjour*. Can you tell me where Nykki lives?" Elizabeth asked.

The boy looked up at her and giggled shyly, then pointed toward a road that branched off to the left.

"How far?" she asked.

The boy just giggled some more. *He's probably never heard anyone who speaks like me*, Elizabeth thought. "Which house is it?" She formed her French words slowly, paying careful attention to her accent.

The other boy approached them. He looked slightly older. "It's the enormous house." He pointed down the same road. "There aren't any others that way."

Elizabeth thanked the two little boys, letting them pat Nykki for a few moments longer. Then she started off in the direction they had indicated. The road twisted and turned for a few minutes, winding through wooded land. Then it straightened out and opened up. At the very end, a huge, sprawling villa rose out of lush, geometric gardens. There was a central building, with a wing attached to each side. To the left of the structure was a lake surrounded by tall, dark, slender cypress trees.

"Wow!" Elizabeth exclaimed.

Nykki barked happily and started running toward the large house. Elizabeth jogged after him, out of breath by the time she arrived at the front door. She hesitated a moment, then picked up the heavy brass knocker, letting it fall back down with a loud, dull thud.

She heard footsteps, and then the door was pulled open by a small, dark-haired woman wearing a crisp, white, lace-trimmed apron over a black frock. The housekeeper. *"Oui?"* she asked, as Nykki bounded past her and disappeared inside the cavernous house.

"Nykki. Is he yours?" Elizabeth questioned in French.

"He belongs to the Countess de Willenich," the woman replied in French. "This is her home. Is there anything I can help you with?"

Elizabeth began to explain that Nykki had followed her and that she wanted to return him, but she got her words mixed up, and the sentence came out hopelessly scrambled. The housekeeper raised her eyebrows.

"Jacqueline, who's there?" called a voice in French from inside.

Elizabeth was flustered. "The dog," she called back in French. "He wanted to stay with me."

"I'll be right there," the voice said. A second later, a slender old woman swept gracefully down the front hall. "Hello." She approached

Elizabeth, smiled warmly, and extended her hand. "I'm the Countess de Willenich."

"My name is Elizabeth Wakefield. I'm a visitor to Cannes. I was taking a walk and—"

"Nykki decided he had found a friend. Is that it?"

Elizabeth nodded. "He's adorable. And so friendly."

The countess laughed. "And he shows good taste, befriending such a charming young lady." She switched easily into fluent English.

"I thank you so much for bringing my puppy home," the countess continued. "I was beginning to worry about him. But come in, my dear, and let me show you my appreciation. May I offer you something to drink? A glass of wine, perhaps?"

"That's very nice of you, but you really don't have to."

"My dear, I insist. I'd like to express my gratitude. Nykki is like my baby now that my own two children are grown up and have families of their own. Besides, I'm delighted to have a foreign visitor." Countess de Willenich took Elizabeth's arm and led her down the long hallway. "Is this your first trip to France?" she inquired.

Elizabeth nodded, awed by the grandeur of the room she entered with the countess. Antique furniture filled the spacious, airy room, and two portraits hung on the far wall. One appeared to be the countess at a younger age, serene in a black evening dress. A diamond choker sparkled against her smooth skin. The other painting was of a handsome, jet-haired man in a tuxedo.

"My husband, the Count de Willenich," the countess said. "We sat for portraits shortly after we were married." She gestured toward the plush velvet couch across from the paintings. "Why don't you make yourself comfortable right here, Elizabeth? I'll have Jacqueline bring us some wine. Do you prefer red or white?"

Elizabeth blushed as she sat down. Back in Sweet Valley, she almost never drank wine. Her parents might let her and Jessica have a glass with dinner, but only on very special occasions. The last time had been when her mother had picked up an important new client for her design business.

But here in France, having a glass of wine seemed to be as common as opening a can of Coke. Even the younger children drank wine, although it was mixed with water. "I'll have whatever you have," Elizabeth told the countess. "Just half a glass, please."

"We have a lovely red from one of the local vineyards," the countess said. "Jacqueline, could you bring in some of the Château Marcelline?"

Jacqueline nodded from the doorway.

The countess turned back to Elizabeth. "Have

you seen any of the vineyards yet?" she asked as she sat down next to her.

"Well, actually, I just got here yesterday," Elizabeth explained. "I haven't had a chance to see much, although I had coffee at the Festival Café this afternoon and ate lunch in a nice little restaurant off on one of the side streets."

"Two days in Cannes and you've already been to the Festival? My dear, I'd say you're doing quite well!" The countess smiled. "That's quite the place to go."

"I'm looking forward to seeing more of the sights," Elizabeth remarked. "I was reading about the great view from the Cannes observatory, and the Castre Museum."

"Oh, yes, the observatory view is wonderful, and the museum is quite interesting, also, but a young girl like you—I'd think your top priority would be the beaches and the clubs." The old woman launched into a description of the various beaches in and around Cannes, and the best spots to go after the sun went down.

Elizabeth settled back on the couch, taking the glass of wine Jacqueline brought her. This was proving to be a wonderful afternoon after all. René could keep all his mean remarks and hateful glances. Elizabeth had made her first friend in Cannes. And she hadn't needed him to do it.

"She was so much fun to talk to. Really young

at heart, if you know what I mean," Elizabeth said. "And guess what? She invited me back tomorrow for tea!"

"And you're going?" Jessica helped herself to a third serving of green beans with a delicate lemon-butter sauce, and another half a piece of tender bifteck au poivre, a steak with a pepper-seasoned coating. If Avery kept making such incredible meals, Jessica thought, they were going to have to roll her off the plane when she got back to Sweet Valley.

"Of course I'm going. Why wouldn't I?" Elizabeth asked. "In fact, I can't wait till tomorrow afternoon."

"Well, frankly, Liz, I could think of more exciting things to do than spending a gorgeous day inside, talking to some old lady." Jessica took a big mouthful of beans.

"Jessica Wakefield! The countess is a really neat woman! It'll be a pleasure to talk to her again."

"The countess is also one of the most important women in France," Avery put in. "It's a real honor to be a guest of hers. I've heard she loves talking with foreigners. She's lived all over the world, and I think she speaks four or five languages."

"Six," Elizabeth corrected. "If you count sign language as one of them. The countess told me that her best friend when she was growing up was deaf, so she learned to speak with her hands. She's a fascinating woman."

Jessica shrugged. "Maybe so, but I'll take the beach club any day. You know I met so many people, I couldn't even keep track of who was who." They had spent most of the meal talking about Elizabeth's countess. Now it was Jessica's turn. She neglected to add that most of the people she'd met were friends of Marc's parents and about as exciting as an afternoon at the dentist, but she felt it couldn't hurt to let everyone think she'd had the time of her life. Especially René. She would show him that she could manage an absolutely fantastic vacation without the slightest bit of assistance.

"So the beach was as beautiful as everyone says?" Elizabeth asked, helping to stack the dishes after everyone was finished and passing them to Avery, who took them into the kitchen.

"Even better. Oh, and, Liz, I've been dying to tell you this all day. Most of the women don't wear bathing suit tops. Can you believe it! You can get just about an all-over tan! No strap marks to worry about or anything."

Jessica had tried acting nonchalant at the beach, but it had taken the better part of the morning before she'd felt comfortable enough to join the rest of the crowd. "When in Rome, do as the Romans do," she had joked to Marc with some embarrassment, when she had finally removed her tiny top. Then she'd immediately made a dive for the beach blanket, lying down flat on her stomach.

"Well, you know we Europeans are more comfortable with our bodies than you Americans," René remarked haughtily, now that his mother was out of the room. He had been almost civil during the meal, and Jessica suspected that his mother was holding some punishment over his head if he didn't show his visitors a touch of courtesy. But the second Avery was out of earshot, the twins again became the objects of René's verbal target practice.

Jessica could feel herself growing more and more angry. "For your information, René, I've never had any complaints about my shape. You're the first."

"That's not what I meant," René protested irritably. "You girls are champions at twisting people's words, aren't you?"

"I wasn't aware that I had even said anything," Elizabeth jumped in. "But correct me if I'm wrong, René. I'm sure that would give you great pleasure."

"You tell him, Liz," said Jessica. Her twin rarely lost her temper, but when she did, it was for a good reason. That jerk René must have really given Elizabeth a hard time that afternoon, Jessica thought. Just one more reason why he was at the top of Jessica's ten-worst list.

René turned to Elizabeth, his green eyes blazing. "Tell me, Liz, what difference does it make whether you said something or Jessica did?" He didn't wait for an answer. "You're two of a kind," he rushed on. "All you American girls are the same."

Jessica would have laughed if she hadn't been so angry. She and Elizabeth might look like images of each other, but that was where the resemblance ended. Anyone could see that. It appeared as though René couldn't see beyond the chip on his shoulder when it came to Americans.

The bickering might have gone on indefinitely had Avery not reentered the room with a luscious-looking apple tart and a dish of crème fraîche, a heavenly French treat that was something like a cross between whipped and sour cream.

Suddenly René was as sugary as the dessert his mother was putting on the table. "Here, Mother, let me help you." He took the small plates his mother was holding and passed them around. "No, you sit back and let me serve. You worked all day and then came home and made a wonderful dinner. You should have a chance to relax."

Jessica didn't intend to be outdone by René's Mr. Wonderful act. "Yes, Avery, dinner was superb. Everything they say about French cooking is true. I feel very lucky to be a guest in your home."

"Well, thank you, Jessica. Aren't you sweet."

Jessica smiled demurely at Avery Glize. Then she caught René's eye and flashed him one of her fake toothy grins. Two could play this little game. But the second time René's mother turned to get some small forks from the cupboard behind her, Jessica's grin turned into a scowl. René was her enemy. And she was going to make sure he knew she despised him every bit as much as he despised her.

Seven

Countess de Willenich opened the door herself. "Ah, Elizabeth, how nice to see you again! Come right in." She kissed her on both cheeks.

Elizabeth followed her down the now familiar hallway, her shoes clicking on the ornately glazed ceramic tiles. As she passed the staircase leading up to the second floor, she heard a bark, followed by a furry blur speeding down the stairs. She crouched down to greet Nykki, and he jumped up on her with such force that she almost lost her balance. He sprang onto his hind legs and planted a wet slurp across her nose.

"Hello, my friend!" Elizabeth said happily. "Yes, I'm glad to see you, too." She patted his head. "Countess, you have quite a frisky puppy here."

"I certainly do, but I'm afraid I'm going to have to start training him to hold back a bit. He's eventually going to be twice that size. Can you imagine the strength he's going to have then?" The countess gave Nykki an affectionate pat and then ushered Elizabeth into the room in which she had entertained her the day before.

There on the couch sat a young man with sandy brown hair, large, wide-set eyes and strong, chiseled features. He stood up as soon as Elizabeth and the countess entered the room. He was tall and well-built, his body a deep tan against his tennis whites. He smiled broadly.

"Oh, Jean-Claude, I didn't realize you were home," the countess said to him with surprise. "Elizabeth, this is my grandson, Jean-Claude de Willenich. He's staying with me for a few weeks. Jean-Claude, Elizabeth Wakefield." The countess addressed him in French. "She's the young American who brought Nykki home yesterday. She's come to have tea with me. You're welcome to join us if you'd like."

"*Bonjour*, Jean-Claude. Nice to meet you," Elizabeth said.

"*Bonjour*, Elizabeth," Jean-Claude said, coming forward and shaking her hand. "*Enchanté*. So very glad to make your acquaintance." He switched into English, forming the words with difficulty and laboring over each syllable.

"I'm afraid that's one of Jean-Claude's only English phrases," the countess explained.

"Yes. My father insisted I learn it for when he and Mother entertain foreign diplomats, that sort of thing," Jean-Claude said offhandedly, speaking French again. "But I much prefer to use it on beautiful blond American girls." His eyes twinkled.

"I assume that means you'll join us for tea, Jean-Claude," the countess said wryly.

"Yes, of course, as long as Elizabeth doesn't mind practicing her French."

"Oh, not at all," Elizabeth responded in French. "In fact, I'm happy to have a chance to use it. That is one of the reasons why I'm here in Cannes." She had to keep her words simple but was happy to find the language was beginning to come more easily and naturally.

Elizabeth had watched a movie on television the night before and had learned more in two hours than she had in two months of French classes back in Sweet Valley. Actually, she had gotten the most out of the commercials. They were easier to follow than the features and came in fifteen-minute to half-hour blocks before and after the programs in order not to interrupt them. Elizabeth thought this system made a lot of sense.

At breakfast Elizabeth had read a French newspaper while she was having her morning coffee and croissant. There were many words

89

she hadn't understood, but she had gotten the gist of most of the articles.

Her sentences flowed more smoothly than they had only two days before. Jean-Claude wanted to know if everything he had heard about California was true, and Elizabeth was trying to sort out fact from fiction for him.

"Do they really have hot tubs in every house?" he wanted to know. "And women to share them with? I think I'd like a place like that." The countess had laughingly translated the French word for hot tub. "And what about movie stars and famous rock musicians? A friend of mine said all you have to do to see them is go to a fancy club or restaurant."

"What else do they teach you about us?" Elizabeth giggled. "Next thing you know they'll be saying that we Californians have pointy ears and green skin!" *Or worse*, she added to herself, recalling René's opinion of her for one sobering moment.

But why waste time moping about that boy when she had found somebody who was friendly and open? She willed René out of her mind and refocused her attention on Jean-Claude.

"To answer your questions, the only person I know with a hot tub is a girl at school, Lila Fowler, although a boy at school, Bruce Patman, just got a new Swedish sauna out by his pool." Elizabeth told Jean-Claude and the countess about Bruce's most recent pool party, when they'd steamed up in the sauna and then jumped straight into the brisk water under a star-studded sky. "I guess that's a pretty California kind of party. As for the actors and musicians, most of them are in Los Angeles. I've visited there, and actually I did see some famous people once, when we went out to this really hot new club. It was wild! There they were, dancing right next to us!"

"So in other words, everything they say about California is true, if you know where to look," Jean-Claude observed.

"I guess that's one way of putting it," Elizabeth answered. "It's kind of like the impressions that we grow up with about France. I suppose I was expecting to see hundreds of old men walking around in berets, and artists painting on every street corner. You can find them, of course, but most of the people are, well, more like—"

"Like ordinary men and women?" Jean-Claude laughed.

"Well, yes. Except there are certain differences. The shoes, for instance, and the way French people dress. They have a different style than we do. All the girls here wear tight jeans with heels and long, bulky sweaters. And glittery scarves." Elizabeth thought about all the clothing Jessica had wanted to buy as soon as

91

she'd had a day to see what the French girls were wearing.

"And you and your friends, you prefer Levis and jogging clothes?" Jean-Claude wondered. "But how silly of me, there you are in a stunning outfit—"

"Oh, thank you," Elizabeth said. Stunning wasn't exactly the word she would have chosen for her comfortably worn blue sun dress, but she appreciated Jean-Claude's compliment. "Actually, we do wear sports clothes a lot, but even when we don't, it's a different look from what I've seen here. It's hard to describe the difference, though."

"Yes, that's true," the countess put in. "After traveling as much as I have, I find I can usually tell a person's nationality simply by looking at him or her."

"Countess, how wonderful it must be to have seen so much of the world! There are so many places I'd like to visit." Elizabeth helped herself to a biscuit to go with the delicious blackberry tea the countess had poured for her. "Although right now I'll settle for Cannes!"

"Elizabeth, now that you've mentioned it, would you like me to take you around to see our city?" Jean-Claude asked. "I've spent part of every summer here since I was a small boy, and I love to show it off to people. Especially people like you." He winked.

Elizabeth laughed. Jean-Claude was what

Jessica would call a charmer. Perhaps a bit too much of the lady's man for Elizabeth's taste, but he was handsome, nice, and, no denying it, fabulously wealthy. That last item didn't make much difference to her, but she could almost hear Jessica's voice, telling her she'd be a fool not to accept a date with a guy like this.

"Yes, I'd love you to show me around, Jean-Claude."

"Wonderful." The countess clapped her hands. "You two young people go ahead."

"Oh, but, countess, I did come to visit you," Elizabeth said, feeling uncomfortable about leaving the older woman to go off with someone she'd just met. "Why don't Jean-Claude and I stay and talk with you this afternoon? We can see the sights tomorrow." Yes, that was a good solution.

"Nonsense. You go right ahead."

Jean-Claude took his cue from Elizabeth. "Are you certain you don't want us to stay, Grandmother?"

"Absolutely. If I had wanted Elizabeth all to myself, I never would have introduced her to you," the countess said lightly. She looked from her grandson to Elizabeth, then back to her grandson. "Besides, I have a hunch that I'll be seeing our lovely visitor quite a bit." She sat back in her antique armchair, an expression of satisfaction on her face.

Why, she planned this whole thing, Elizabeth

93

thought. Here she was, pretending that she didn't know Jean-Claude was home, while in truth she had probably been plotting this "accidental" meeting since the minute she'd invited Elizabeth back for tea! Well, Elizabeth had wanted a friend to show her around, and now it seemed that she had one.

Jean-Claude pulled up in front of the Glizes, at the end of the day. "This is it, isn't it? I was here last summer when René had a party."

Elizabeth felt her temper rise like a helium balloon at the mention of René's name, but she tried not to let it show. There was no reason to involve Jean-Claude in her feud with René. "Yes, this is it," she said, outwardly calm.

Jean-Claude put the Citroen in park.

"Thank you, Jean-Claude. I had a lovely afternoon." Elizabeth slung the strap of her bag over her shoulder.

"It was my pleasure."

"That view from the observatory was incredible."

"And don't forget *boules*."

Boules was a sport similar to American lawn bowling. The object was to toss grapefruit-sized metal balls toward a smaller ball, coming as close to the small ball as possible. Elizabeth had noticed a group of older men playing it, and when she had asked Jean-Claude about it, he'd insisted on explaining all the finer points of this national pastime to her. He had even asked the men to let her shoot a couple of balls.

"Yes, *boules* was fun," Elizabeth said. "But if I had managed to roll those bigger balls any farther from the little one, they would have gone right off the playing area. I think I ought to stick to tennis."

"You play tennis? Wonderful. Perhaps we can play tomorrow," Jean-Claude suggested. "Or would you rather go to the beach? A friend of mine is supposed to be there later in the day with his motorboat, so we could water ski if you'd like. I mean, if you want to do something together," he added with a little laugh.

It occurred to Elizabeth that Jean-Claude wasn't really worried about being turned down. He was like Jessica in that way. They both had a kind of casual confidence that made Elizabeth feel shy by comparison.

Not that Jean-Claude's attitude was hard to understand. Elizabeth had found him intelligent and good company. Add that to his looks and the fact that he was from one of the best families in France, and she could see why he might feel sure of himself. He was also Elizabeth's only friend in Cannes, and she was grateful for his invitation.

"So what will it be? Tennis or the beach?" he asked again.

"Well, I still haven't gone swimming in the Mediterranean," Elizabeth said.

"Then we'll have to do something about that," Jean-Claude replied, smiling.

"Great. I was afraid I might spend my whole vacation in Cannes without ever getting into the water."

"Yes, well, I can understand why René might not want to take you," Jean-Claude mused.

"What do you know about that?" Elizabeth burst out involuntarily.

Jean-Claude looked puzzled. "Didn't René tell you?"

"Tell me what?" Elizabeth tried to control herself. It was absurd to let René get to her when she wasn't even with him.

Jean-Claude's sunny, relaxed manner gave way to a gloomy expression. "It's a sad story. I'm surprised no one's told you yet. Everyone in Cannes heard about it when it happened."

"Heard about what?"

"There was an accident several summers ago. René's best friend died." Jean-Claude shook his head.

"Oh, no. What happened?" Elizabeth asked, almost afraid to hear the answer.

"They were swimming together. René was out in front. He's a very strong swimmer. I mean he was . . . He used to race on the junior team here and was a lifeguard during the summer. Anyway, René was way ahead, swimming with his head underwater, when his friend developed a cramp. René stopped to look behind him, and his friend was yelling for help. René said later that he didn't know when his friend began calling. He didn't hear anything until he lifted his head out of the water."

Jean-Claude took a deep breath. "Anyway, by the time he got back to where his friend was, the guy was already under. René kept diving down. On his third dive he saw him, but he had to come up for air. When he went back down again, his friend was lost. They sent out a search party, but it was too late."

"Oh, no." Elizabeth put her hands to her face.

"René watched them drag his friend's body out of the sea," Jean-Claude finished. "He hasn't gone in the water since then."

"Poor René." An oasis of sympathy sprang up in the desert of anger that Elizabeth had felt. What a nightmare to live through. She wished with all her heart that she hadn't asked René to take her to the beach the day before. She couldn't excuse his behavior in general, but on that particular point, he certainly had a reason for flaring up the way he had. He probably felt responsible for his friend's death. Elizabeth couldn't think of anything worse than that.

Her concern for René battled with her resentment at his inhospitality. She felt much the way she had when René's friends had confirmed her suspicions about his father. One part of her wanted to try to talk to René, to tell him she understood; the other, more realistic part told her to forget about bringing him around. That it was hopeless. Elizabeth sighed. Why was it so complicated?

"Elizabeth? Are you all right?" Jean-Claude's voice broke into her thoughts.

"Oh, yes, I'm sorry. It's just the story. How awful." She shook her head, her blond ponytail swinging from side to side.

"It was. But it was a long time ago." Jean-Claude switched on the car radio, breaking the somber mood. "So, how about if I pick you up around twelve-thirty tomorrow?"

Elizabeth made herself smile. "That sounds fine. Well, thanks again for a very nice time."

Jean-Claude leaned over and gave Elizabeth a quick kiss on her right cheek, followed by another on her left. "See you then. And, Elizabeth, cheer up. There's nothing you can do about it." He patted her hand.

Elizabeth let herself out of the car and gave a little wave as Jean-Claude drove off. But she couldn't shake the image of René struggling to save his friend's life, or stop imagining the expression in his green eyes when they dragged his friend out of the sea.

Elizabeth thought about her own best friend, Enid Rollins, and how horrible it had been when her life had been endangered in the crash landing of her boyfriend's small plane. Elizabeth couldn't imagine how she would have felt if Enid had died. Thank goodness she was safe and sound back in Sweet Valley, Elizabeth told herself, giving a shiver of relief and crossing her fingers just to make extra sure.

Enid was indeed safe and sound. But she was also very worried. Worried about Cara Walker. Cara was sitting alone, picking at a dish of ice cream when Enid walked into Casey's. She had dark circles under her big brown eyes, which were ringed with red as if she'd been crying. Her face was pale, and she sat slumped over the counter.

"Cara?" Enid walked over and took the stool next to her.

"Enid. Hi." Cara's voice was listless. "You want this? I thought I should eat something, but I guess I'm not really hungry. It's vanilla swiss almond," she added, making a weak attempt to be more cheerful.

"No, thanks. I just came in here for something to drink on the way to my baby-sitting job. But why aren't you eating it? Cara, what's the matter?"

"Oh, don't worry about me, Enid. I'm fine. Really. Go ahead and get what you came in for, and go on to work. I don't want to make you late."

"I've got plenty of time. I don't have to be

there for another twenty minutes." Enid put a hand on Cara's shoulder. "You look like you could use a friend."

Cara stirred her plastic spoon around in the ice-cream dish. "I guess that's true."

"It's Steve, isn't it?" Enid spoke gently. She and Cara had had their differences, but Cara had changed a great deal recently. Besides, Enid felt very strongly that when someone needed you, you made certain to be there.

"How'd you know?" Cara pushed a strand of dark brown hair out of her face and rubbed her eyes.

"I saw him at the beach the other day."

"And she was with him?"

Enid nodded. "The way she looks—well, it must be difficult for everyone."

Cara nodded and swallowed hard. "He hasn't left her side for a second. And he hasn't been returning my phone calls. That's how crazy he is about that girl." A single tear rolled down her cheek. "Enid, it's so unfair. Just when we were so happy together."

"Well, what are you going to do about it?" Enid asked.

"Do? I'm not going to do anything. There's nothing I can do." Cara shook her head, despair and pain shadowing her pretty face.

"You can fight, Cara." Enid's words were soft, but she meant them from the bottom of her soul.

"It just won't work to fight, Enid," Cara said. She bit her lip. "You can't fight the dead."

"You're not fighting the dead. That's exactly it," Enid said. "It's not Tricia who's your competition. She only looks like her. That's what you have to make Steve see. You have to make him realize that Ferney just represents a memory he's holding on to."

"A memory he has every reason to cherish."

"Yes, that's true, but you can't go out with a memory."

Cara gave a bitter laugh. "Try telling Steve that. You know, it was so hard for him after Tricia died. It took a long time for him just to get to the point where he didn't feel guilty about going on dates with other girls. He knew Tricia would have wanted him to, but he felt as if he were doing something wrong."

Cara toyed with a strand of hair, twisting it around her index finger. "But you know, Enid, I thought he'd gotten over that. I thought he was ready to love somebody again. I guess I made a mistake."

"I don't think so. Cara, don't give up."

"Enid, it's really nice of you to try and make me feel better. It means a lot to me, but the only thing for me to do is to try to forget about Steve once and for all. Look, you'd better get going, or you'll be late."

Enid glanced at her watch. "You're right, but are you going to be all right?"

"I'll be fine." Cara nodded, but she was clearly holding back a flood of tears.

"Well, if you need someone to talk to, give me a call," Enid said as she stood up.

"Yeah, and thanks, Enid."

"Anytime." Enid gave her a pat on the back and went over to the other side of the ice cream parlor to order a 7-Up. As she was leaving, she looked over at Cara one last time. Cara's head was down, her hair falling in front of her face. She was still stirring her spoon in its dish, around and around in a mechanical motion.

Eight

"I can't wait for Jean-Claude to pick me up for the beach," Elizabeth said. "Isn't it terrific, Jess? Now we both have friends here."

"Yeah, terrific," Jessica returned flatly. They were standing outside on the balcony of their room, and Jessica stared at the water, not really seeing it. She couldn't believe it. Elizabeth had met the gorgeous, rich grandson of a count and countess, while she was stuck with nerdy little Marc.

"You don't sound that happy about it." Elizabeth gave a little frown. "Is something wrong, Jess?"

"Wrong? What could be wrong?"

"I don't know. You tell me."

"Oh, Liz, it's nothing." Jessica avoided her sister's probing gaze. "I guess I was still thinking of what you told me about René and that friend of his who drowned," she lied.

Actually, she couldn't have cared less. René didn't deserve an ounce of her sympathy. But she couldn't tell Elizabeth what she was really feeling. What would she say? That she thought *she* should have been the one to hook up with a rich, important, good-looking guy? But it was true. After all, Elizabeth didn't even think about things like titles and money, and she'd said herself that she didn't know if she was quite ready for a new romance. Jean-Claude's looks would only be wasted on her.

"Yeah, that drowning was horrible for me to hear about, too." Elizabeth shook her head. "I feel sorry for René, even though he hasn't been the nicest host." She paused. "But anyway, now it looks like I'll have Jean-Claude to show me around, so René won't have to. Maybe one day we could even go to the same beach—you and Marc and Jean-Claude and I," Elizabeth continued on a happier note. "I'd like you to meet him."

Jessica brightened a little. "Yeah, that would be great. I'd like to meet him, too." *Boy, would I like to meet him,* she added to herself.

"I think you'd get along well," Elizabeth remarked. "In fact, Jess, that thought kept

104

occurring to me when he was showing me around yesterday.''

"Really?" Jessica kept her tone casual, but she was growing more intrigued about Jean-Claude by the moment. "Well, um, did you tell him about me?" She hopped up on the railing of the balcony.

"I told him I was here with my sister. I couldn't remember the word for twin, though.''

"Jumelle," Jessica supplied a bit smugly. *"Jumeau,* for boys." This was a first—translating a word for Elizabeth.

A look of pleasant surprise crossed Elizabeth's face. "Hey, where'd you learn that?''

"Oh, Marc, I guess. You know, I'm really starting to pick things up. Last night, I even had part of a dream in French. But where were we?'' Jessica was more interested in Jean-Claude than in discussing her new vocabulary. "Oh, yes, your new friend. Maybe I could meet him today. What time is he coming by?''

"Twelve-thirty. But, Jess, I thought you were going to the beach with Marc at ten-thirty.''

"I can always cancel my plans.''

"Marc would be so disappointed,'' Elizabeth said. "Don't do that, Jessica. You'll meet Jean-Claude another time.''

"When?''

Elizabeth gave Jessica a funny look. "What's the rush? I thought Marc was introducing you to all kinds of fascinating people.''

Jessica could feel Elizabeth's penetrating stare. She gazed off in the distance, across the rolling vista to where the yachts were docked, not meeting her twin's eyes. "Oh, he is," she replied.

"So why would you want to cancel your plans with him?" Elizabeth questioned.

Jessica had so embellished her stories about Marc and his beach club that now she was trapped. "All right, so I'll meet your fabulous guy some other time," she said irritably. "Listen, Liz, I'd better go if I don't want to be late."

"Have fun," Elizabeth said.

"Sure." Jessica went inside, grabbed her beach things, and rushed out of the house. *Sure, I'll have fun, letting Marc fawn all over me while you go off with Mr. Extraordinary*, she thought, feeling sorry for herself. It wasn't supposed to work out this way. Elizabeth wasn't even trying to meet any fabulous guys, yet she was the one who'd ended up with Jean-Claude. It wasn't fair. Jessica wanted a piece of the action. And somehow, she was going to make sure she got it.

Elizabeth changed into her blue-and-green bikini, topped with a pair of shorts and an oversized shirt. She folded a towel and packed it in her beach bag along with a book and a tube of suntan lotion. Then she went downstairs to wait for Jean-Claude.

The house was quiet. Avery had left for work

before Elizabeth had woken up. René had left after breakfast, not bothering to say where he was going.

The silence was broken by the sharp ring of the telephone. Elizabeth raced into the kitchen and picked up the receiver after the third double-ring. *"Allô?"* she said, mimicking the way she'd heard Avery and René answering their phone calls.

"Liz? Jessica?"

"It's Liz. Avery?"

"Yes. Hello, dear. May I speak to René?"

"He's not home. He left a while ago."

"Oh, no," Avery moaned. "Did he say when he was coming back?"

"No, he didn't." Elizabeth could detect a note of frenzy in Avery's voice. "Is something wrong?"

Avery let out a breath of exasperation. "I'm afraid I'm having a little emergency here. The doctor has ordered medication for my patient, but the druggist can't deliver it."

"Is there any way I can get it to you?" Elizabeth volunteered.

"Oh, Liz, I hate to bother you, but I can't do without it, and I also can't leave this woman alone."

"Is there a bus I could take to get to where you are?" Elizabeth asked. "Maybe I could stop at the pharmacy and bring the medicine to you."

"I'd be so grateful. Liz, you're a doll."

"No problem, Avery." Elizabeth glanced at her watch. "Do you think I can be back by twelve-thirty? I'm meeting Jean-Claude here."

"Well, you'll have to walk down to the valley to catch the bus. I believe there's one every half hour." Avery thought out loud. "It might take something like an hour and a half. Perhaps you could leave Jean-Claude a note on the door and ask him to wait a few minutes. Oh, I'm so sorry—"

"It's all right, Avery. I'm sure he'll wait." Elizabeth tore a sheet of paper from the note pad near the telephone and found a pencil. "Just tell me how to get there and where to get the medicine."

Avery's relief was evident in her voice. "I don't know what I'd do without you." she said gratefully. "I'll reimburse you when you arrive. You can catch a bus into the center of Cannes at the bottom of the hill, and the pharmacy is right across the street from the last stop. Then you connect to another bus to get here."

Avery proceeded to give her complete directions, and Elizabeth wrote them down as carefully as she could. It might actually be fun to try to get around Cannes on her own, she thought.

She assured Avery that she'd be there as soon as possible and said goodbye, replacing the receiver in its cradle. She ran back upstairs and quickly got some French francs, inspecting the strange-looking bills and coins as she dropped them into her purse. The paper money came in different colors and sizes, depending on the denomination. Jean-Claude had shown her how to see the watermark on each one by holding it up to the light.

She wrote a note to Jean-Claude, saying she'd be back by twelve-thirty, taped it to the outside of the door, and locked up behind her. She was certain that Jean-Claude would understand if she was a few minutes late.

Jessica sighed loudly, turned over onto her back, and sighed again. Here she was, stuck on this boring strip of beach, surrounded by a bunch of boring people, while Elizabeth was getting ready to go off with the grandson of a countess.

"Jessica, is anything wrong?" Marc asked, his brown eyes warm with concern.

"Would you stop asking me that?" Jessica snapped. "I just have sort of a headache, OK?"

"I'm sorry. Perhaps it is the heat. A swim would make you feel better."

"No, it's not the heat." Jessica imitated his accent testily. Why didn't this guy stop bugging her, just for a second? It was all Elizabeth's fault for talking her into another boring day with Marc. She should have insisted on canceling her plans instead of listening to her twin.

"A cold drink?" Marc was ready to jump right

up and run over to the café nestled on the edge of the sand.

"No. That won't help."

Marc bit his lower lip. "Do you want to go home?" he asked hesitantly. "If you don't feel well—"

That was the best idea he'd had all morning. In fact, thought Jessica, stealing a peek at Marc's watch, if they hurried, she might even get home before Jean-Claude arrived to pick her sister up. He might be occupied with Elizabeth, but maybe he had some friends who'd be more her speed than Marc was.

"Yes, maybe I should go home," Jessica said demurely.

Marc looked so let down that Jessica almost couldn't stand it. "Look, we'll do something again soon." Now that she was off the hook, it was easier to be generous. She even managed a little half-smile.

Marc stood up and extended his hand to Jessica. She allowed him to help her up. Within minutes, they were in his Porsche, cruising back up one of the roads that led to the Glizes' house.

"How is your head?" Marc inquired anxiously, gently steering the car around a bend.

Jessica could see by his watch that it was nearly twelve-thirty. If they didn't hurry, Jean-Claude and Elizabeth might be gone before she got back. "My head is really pounding." She brought one hand to her forehead in a dramatic gesture. "Maybe we could go a little faster. I really need to take some aspirin and get into bed."

Marc obligingly stepped on the gas pedal. Soon the white walls of the house were in sight.

"Thanks, Marc. And, look, I'm sorry if I messed up your plans for the day." Jessica gathered her things and got out of the car.

"Feel better, Jessica," said Marc. She could feel his eyes on her as she turned and went up the front walk. It wasn't until she reached the front door that she heard the Porsche take off.

Whew! Marc was out of her hair for a while, she thought with relief. It was true that he was awfully sweet, but sweet was simply not enough. She wasn't going to be in Cannes long enough to waste another day being bored out of her skull, and by now it was obvious that Marc was not going to help her meet the kind of people she was looking for. Jean-Claude, on the other hand, might.

She took out the key Avery had given her and raised it to the keyhole. It was then that she noticed the piece of paper taped to the door. She read it, feeling a tingle of pleasure as she realized that she'd have awhile to entertain Jean-Claude before her twin got back. How convenient. Now she would have a chance to see if he was really everything Elizabeth said he was.

Jessica pulled down the note and stuffed it into her beach bag. No reason to leave it up, she decided. She'd be here to tell Jean-Claude in person that her sister had gone on an emergency errand.

Once inside, she raced up to her room, brushed her hair, pulled her short, red T-shirt dress on over her bathing suit, and then went out to the living room to wait.

At exactly twelve-thirty there was a knock at the door. The guy was nothing if not prompt, Jessica thought. She straightened her dress, walked over to the front door, and pulled it open.

She almost gasped as she took her first look at Jean-Claude. Elizabeth had said he was handsome, but she hadn't prepared Jessica for somebody who could take her breath away.

Jean-Claude was tall and muscular, his skin burnished to a deep golden tan. His sandy hair was streaked with blond, and a lock of it fell across his model-perfect face. His eyes were light brown, almost amber, and they held her gaze so intently that Jessica felt as if she were drowning.

"*Salut*," he greeted her. His voice was deep and melodic, his smile warm. "*Ça va*, Elizabeth?" He asked how she was.

Hearing her twin's name was a slap of reality for Jessica. She tried to pull herself together and explain to Jean-Claude that she was not who he thought she was. "You've made a mistake," she began in French. It was suddenly more difficult than ever for Jessica to put together a sentence.

She fought to think clearly through the haze of giddiness that she felt as she gazed up at Jean-Claude. Forget being introduced to his *friends*. This was the guy she wanted.

"What do you mean?" he asked, his face puzzled. "We did say twelve-thirty, didn't we?"

"Yes, but—"

"But what?" asked Jean-Claude, adding something that Jessica didn't quite catch.

"Excuse me?" Jessica had to ask him to repeat himself.

"I wondered if you had changed your mind about going to the beach and waterskiing with me," he said more slowly.

"That's not it. I'd love to go with you," Jessica replied with one-hundred-percent sincerity.

"Well, then, let's go." He took her arm.

Jessica felt a tingle of excitement at his touch. She was ready to let Jean-Claude lead her anywhere. But what about Elizabeth? She couldn't do this to her twin. "Jean-Claude, I have to tell you something."

Jean-Claude was still holding her arm. "Elizabeth, I have to tell *you* something. You look very beautiful today, even more beautiful than yesterday. I don't know what it is. Maybe your hair. I like it loose." He swept a hand through her hair, and Jessica shivered with delight. "Now what was it you wanted to tell me?"

Jessica's thoughts were racing at supersonic

113

speed. What if she did go with Jean-Claude? Elizabeth thought he was nice, but she wasn't absolutely wild about him. *Not the way I am,* Jessica told herself. She had never met anyone she felt so instantly attracted to. He was fabulous. Even better than fabulous. And she would never get another chance. It was now or never.

Jessica looked into Jean-Claude's amber-brown eyes, and her head swam. It had to be love at first sight! *If Elizabeth knew how I felt, she'd never stand in my way,* Jessica thought. Besides, Elizabeth had said herself that she thought Jessica would like Jean-Claude. It was Elizabeth who had gotten her interested in meeting him in the first place.

Jean-Claude was still waiting for Jessica to answer him. She made her decision swiftly. "Jean-Claude, I don't remember what I was going to say. I guess it wasn't that important." She grabbed the beach bag she'd flung down by the door when she'd walked in, and gave him her brightest smile. *"Je suis prête.* I'm ready." *Forgive me, Liz,* she added silently.

She and Jean-Claude stepped out into the warm, sweet air. Jessica pulled the door closed behind her, locked it, and they were off.

Nine

Elizabeth sat in the pharmacy, waiting for the medication. She'd been there for more than a half hour, nervously peering over to the drug counter every few minutes to see if her order was ready. She had inspected everything in the store—the French shampoos, the tanning creams and oils, the boxes of strange-looking pills, the soaps scented with fancy perfumes. She had tried on makeup from the sample display. Still her prescription was not ready.

Now she simply stared at her watch as it ticked away. If she didn't hurry, she thought, she'd never be back in time to meet Jean-Claude. When she had started out to do this favor for Avery, Elizabeth had looked on it as a little adventure. But not any longer. It was hot and sunny—a perfect day for waterskiing and swimming in an aqua sea, not for sitting inside a sterile-looking drugstore.

"Mademoiselle Wakefield?" The man behind the counter called her name.

Finally. Elizabeth took the medication from him, counted out the correct amount of money, thanked him, and rocketed out the door. The bus she had to take for the second leg of her trip was pulling up to the curb as she got there. She just made it.

Avery's directions were easy to follow, and within ten minutes Elizabeth was knocking at the door of an old three-story house of brown-gray stone, flanked by several similar houses. Avery opened the door.

"Elizabeth, you don't know how grateful I am. Thank you so much." She took the medication with relief and paid Elizabeth back what she had spent on it.

"You're very welcome," Elizabeth replied, smiling.

"Would you like to come in, have a cup of coffee?" Avery asked.

"No, thanks, Avery, I'm already late getting back to meet Jean-Claude. I'll see you later."

"Yes, I'll be home by dinnertime. And thanks again, Elizabeth."

The first ride back across Cannes went smoothly, and almost before she knew it,

Elizabeth was climbing onto the next bus. But just as she was thinking that she might make it after all, the trip came to a standstill. Less than halfway up the hill leading to the Glizes' house, the bus came upon a line of cars stretched out motionless along the twisting, narrow road. There was no traffic coming down in the opposite direction at all.

"What's happening?" the bus driver called out to one of the numerous people who had gotten out of their cars.

"Accident up ahead," the man replied. He added something else about an argument that was going on, but Elizabeth didn't catch what he'd said.

The bus driver stood up, shook his stocky legs, and turned toward the passengers. "Ladies and gentlemen, it seems we are going to be here for a while. You may leave the bus until we can start moving again, if you wish."

Elizabeth groaned. She didn't have a prayer of getting home by twelve-thirty now. She considered getting out and jogging, but the house was still quite a distance away, and it was all uphill. No matter what she did, she would be very late.

She got out of the bus and walked up the road to investigate. A tiny, mustard-yellow car was angled across both lanes at a bend in the road. It was crushed headlong against a huge tour bus, front fender to front fender. The tour bus had a tiny dent below its left headlight, while the entire hood of the little car was crumpled like an accordion, the windshield shattered.

Apparently the car had skidded around the bend and gone out of control. Its driver and passenger, a young vacationing couple, were bruised and scraped, but miraculously did not have any major injuries. They stood next to their crumpled car, dazed but otherwise all right.

The occupants of the tour bus had drifted out onto the road along with a stream of people from the other vehicles, now backed up in both directions. The tour bus was carrying visitors of various nationalities, and they chattered away in a babble of different languages, discussing the accident, inspecting the damage to the little car, and occasionally offering a few words of reassurance to the unfortunate young couple.

Meanwhile, barbs were being traded by two groups of people gathered around the car. There were too many heated voices yelling at once for Elizabeth to follow what was going on. She turned to a woman next to her and asked what they were saying.

"Oh, do you speak English?" a second woman inquired in a clipped British accent.

Elizabeth nodded. "What are they fighting about?"

"It seems that one group wants to push the car aside so the traffic won't be blocked. The others insist that the police have to arrive first to make a complete report. You know the French. They're rather fond of paperwork."

Elizabeth waved her hand at the crowd. "But there are several dozen witnesses. Surely the police can get a report from some of them without holding the rest of us up." She glanced at her watch. Twenty to one. "This is absurd," she pronounced impatiently.

"Yes, quite," the British woman replied. "But I'm afraid there's nothing to do but wait for the outcome of this debate, unless the police arrive before it's settled."

In the end, one woman broke the deadlock when she noticed that her son had a piece of chalk. It was agreed to mark the spot where the tires had been and to move the car out of traffic. A group of people picked the rear of the car up and swung it around, then pushed the tiny vehicle over to the shoulder of the road.

A cheer went up from the crowd, and people piled back inside the tour bus. Elizabeth sprinted back down to her own bus, taking her seat just as the traffic started flowing. Soon she reached her stop. She flew off the bus and ran up the Glizes' driveway.

But it was too late. The note she'd left was gone. Obviously Jean-Claude had been by, Elizabeth thought, but there was no sign of him. "Oh, no," Elizabeth groaned. She slumped down on the front step. "What a morning."

She felt terrible about standing Jean-Claude

up. It was after one o'clock. She didn't blame him for leaving. She could only hope he wasn't too angry at being kept waiting.

Elizabeth stood up, unlocked the door, and headed for the phone in the kitchen. On it was a sticker listing important numbers. She ran her index finger down it. There. Twelve: *renseignements*—information. She dialed and asked for the Countess de Willenich's number. The operator gave it to her, repeating it twice.

But Jean-Claude was not there, and neither was the countess. Instead, Jacqueline, the housekeeper, answered the telephone. "Can you tell him Elizabeth Wakefield called and ask him to call me back?" Elizabeth asked. She gave Jacqueline the Glizes' phone number, thanked her, and hung up.

So much for an afternoon of waterskiing and the beach, she thought. It looked as if she'd have to wait. But perhaps if Jean-Claude returned her call this evening, they could make it for the next day.

"I meant what I said yesterday about wanting to play tennis with you," Jean-Claude said, as he and Jessica headed for the beach.

"You'd better get ready to play hard," Jessica responded. "I'm hard to beat." Her French came out brokenly, but she got her point across.

"That is what I like—a challenge." Jean-

Claude took one hand off the wheel and clasped Jessica's shoulder. "How about tomorrow morning?"

It was as if every nerve in Jessica's body was channeled to the spot where Jean-Claude's hand met her shoulder. His touch was fire and ice at the same time. "Tomorrow? Yes, of course. Whenever you want," she managed to say.

"Good." Jean-Claude steered to the left, down a different street from the one Marc had taken to the beach.

Jessica was relieved. She didn't want to go anywhere near Marc's beach club, just in case he had gone back after driving her home. To make doubly sure, she asked Jean-Claude exactly where they were going.

"To the beach, of course. I mean I know there's a bit of a language problem between us—maybe even more today than yesterday, it seems—but I thought we were clear on that, at least." He gave an easy laugh.

"All right, all right. Now would you mind telling me which beach?" Jessica's tone was light and flirtatious.

"The lady asks too many questions." Jean-Claude winked at her. "Actually, I'm taking you to the public beach. That is where all the people our age hang out. It is really a lot more fun than some of those exclusive clubs."

Jessica pictured the beach she had gone to with Marc. "Yes, I know exactly what you mean." She nodded. "They can be a real—how do you say it?" She searched her brain for the French word for "drag." It occurred to her that her French wasn't good enough to pass for Elizabeth's. But it was too late to worry about that now. She was too deep into this already. "Well, let's say those beaches can be kind of boring," she improvised.

A confused expression stole over Jean-Claude's handsome features. "I thought you told me you hadn't gone to the beach here yet. What do you mean?"

Jessica thought fast. "Oh—ah—I haven't. I meant, I'd heard from someone that the private clubs can be a little dull," she said, quickly covering up for her mistake.

Jean-Claude's face was still bewildered when he pulled into a parking space across from the beach and turned off the car motor. "Elizabeth, this is going to sound awfully silly, but if I didn't know better, I might be tempted to think you were a different person today."

Jessica cringed as Jean-Claude called her by her twin's name. It really wasn't fair to keep up this masquerade. Perhaps she ought to tell him the truth. Now was her chance. But what if he insisted on turning around and going back for the real Elizabeth? What if Jessica ended up sitting around the house by herself? Worst of all, what if Jean-Claude decided she was a worthless person for fooling him and pulling such a low trick on her sister?

No, Jessica couldn't bear to have Jean-Claude think anything but wonderful thoughts about her. If those thoughts were built on a tiny lie—all right, a not so tiny lie—she'd have to live with it. And besides, what Jean-Claude didn't know wouldn't hurt him, right?

"Jean-Claude, I don't know what you're talking about," she began, the very picture of innocence. "Do I look like a different person from the girl you were with yesterday?" Jessica formed her sentences slowly and carefully. It was of vital importance that he understand her.

"Well, no, of course you don't, although there is something—I don't know—something I find even more attractive about you today. Your spirit, maybe. But that sounds crazy, doesn't it?" Jean-Claude shook his head, looking at her with a confused but intrigued expression.

"You tell me." Jessica cocked her head. "As for my French, I guess I have bad days and good days—just like with anything."

Jean-Claude nodded and reached out for Jessica's hand. "You're right. And you know what? I think this is going to be one of those very good days. For both of us. And I am not talking about speaking French, either." He let his hand brush up her arm, giving her goose bumps all over.

Jessica's gaze lingered on him, drinking him in

with her eyes. Jean-Claude might be mistaken about her identity, but he was absolutely right about one thing. If Jessica Wakefield had anything to say about it, that day was going to be a day to remember forever.

Elizabeth felt miserable. She had just gotten acquainted with Jean-Claude, and already she'd fouled up her plans with him. She sank onto the living room couch and threw her bag down on the floor in annoyance.

"Having a temper tantrum?" A deep voice filled the room.

Elizabeth whirled around. "Oh, René, you scared me. How long have you been home?"

René ignored her question. "And what is it today that's got our American princess so upset?"

"René, please. It's been a difficult morning. I beg you not to start in on me again." Elizabeth clutched at the edge of the couch. René's timing couldn't have been worse.

"What happened? Did you break a fingernail?" René taunted her.

"Look, if you have to know, I've been all the way across Cannes and back to take your mother some medicine for her patient. I've spent a good part of the morning in a drugstore and the rest of it stuck in a traffic jam, and I got back so late that

I missed my date. I don't need you to make things any worse." Elizabeth's voice was tight.

"Oh, you stood Jean-Claude up? Well, I can't say I'm very surprised." René flopped down in the chair across from Elizabeth.

"Just what is that supposed to mean?" Elizabeth's patience had been worn thin even before René began insulting her. Now she was on the brink of exploding.

"My, my, aren't we a bit out of control today? But then you're not used to having people make waves, are you? Life is supposed to be so easy for you. You have everything you need, and you have everything you want, too. And then some. That's what American girls are all about. A closetful of clothes and nothing to wear."

Elizabeth summoned up all her willpower in an attempt to be reasonable. "René, what do you have against me? Have I done anything to you? Has Jessica? Why are you treating us this way?"

"It's not what you've done, it's what you stand for." There was poison in René's words. "All you American girls. You think the sun rises and sets on you alone. That's what they teach you. Oh, we see your movies, get your television shows. I know how you girls think. You let some guy stand outside your door while you take your time getting home. So what? People are supposed to wait for you, aren't they?"

Elizabeth jumped out of her seat, her aqua eyes flashing. "Now listen here, René Glize, and listen well. I did not, I repeat, did not take my time coming back here. I ran as fast as I could all the way from where the bus let me off. And it's not as if I went out for my own amusement. I left because your mother needed me."

"Oh, so now it's my mother's fault."

"No. It's your fault! Your mother called to ask *you* to pick up the medicine. You didn't even tell anyone where you could be reached. Listen, I understand that you have a problem with Americans, but don't make it my problem, too."

"You understand? What do you understand?" René was up out of his seat now, also, his shouts echoing off the living room walls.

Elizabeth took a good look at him. His strong, fine-featured face was red with anger and hostility. He was behaving like a child, not like a young man of nearly eighteen.

She sank back down on the couch. Suddenly it was not René she was angry at, but his father. It was because of him that René still hurt so much and was taking his hurt out on her. "I *do* understand," Elizabeth told him. Her voice was soft now. "René, I know about your father."

The room was as silent as a monastery. René went pale. Elizabeth rushed over to his side. "Are you all right?" She reached out and touched his arm.

As if stung, René jumped back, out of her grasp. The color rushed back into his face, which was twisted into a grimace. "Don't you ever mention my father again. You couldn't possibly understand the first thing about it."

"You're wrong, René. I think I know how painful it must have been, how painful it still is."

"Who are you to talk about pain? You have two parents who love each other and who love you. A perfect family. And you're telling me you know about pain?"

Elizabeth maintained her calm. "I do have a wonderful family. I'm very fortunate in that, and I realize it. But no family is perfect. We have our joys and our sorrows, just as everyone has." She held his gaze with hers. "I'm not saying I've had it rough, but I am saying that I know what it is to ache inside. It must have been a terrible thing that you had to go through. And when I see you hurting, I feel for you. I wouldn't be human if I didn't."

René listened to her, his eyes searching hers as if to determine her sincerity. For a moment he appeared to be softening.

But then the anger and distrust returned to his face. "No, those are just words," he said bitterly. "They're easy to say. It will take more than that to convince me I'm wrong about you." He spun on his heel and stormed out of the room.

Elizabeth watched him go. Why was it so important to her to show him that she wasn't the sort of person he imagined? *Give up,* she told herself. *This is one battle you are not going to win.*

Ten

A continent away, Cara Walker was telling herself the same thing. "It's no use. You can't win," she said aloud, addressing her image in her bedroom mirror. She raised a hand to her face. She was the same person she'd been a week ago—perhaps a bit paler, her eyes puffy from too many nights of fitful sleep—still the girl Steven had held and kissed, the girl he'd said he was falling in love with. How could his feelings have changed so quickly?

Cara swallowed hard, but no tears rolled down her cheeks. She had cried herself out. She was dry inside, empty, numb. She felt as if she were a robot, going through the motions of the day automatically, dead to the sensations of the world around her.

She had told Maria Santelli and Robin Wilson, two friends from the cheer-leading squad, that she'd meet them for pizza at Guido's, but even the thought of a Guido's pie with the works didn't appeal to her that night. She wanted nothing more than to get into bed, pull the covers up over her head, and never come out.

But Maria had been insistent. "You've got to start going out. Show that rat Steven Wakefield that you can have a perfectly good time without him. You're certainly not going to get anywhere staying home and moping all the time. Besides," she'd added, "I'm tired of having one of the biggest mopers in Sweet Valley as a teammate. I want to see you start smiling again."

So Cara had agreed to dinner at Guido's. It was easier than saying no to Maria. She whisked a touch of blush over her cheekbones and brushed her shoulder-length dark brown hair. *No sense looking as lousy as I feel*, she thought. She pulled on a pair of sandals, grabbed her purse, and went out to the living room. Time to face the world.

Her mother, who was watching a movie on television, looked up as she entered the room. "Going out, dear?" She sounded pleased and relieved.

"Yes, I'm meeting Maria and Robin for pizza. I

wondered if I could borrow the Honda. If not, Robin said she'd drive over and pick me up."

Her mother stood up and reached into her skirt pocket. "Here, honey." She held the car keys out toward Cara. "You have a good time. And drive safely."

Cara took the keys. "Thanks." She wished it were always this easy to borrow the car. Her mother had been so worried about her over the past few days that she'd been ready to offer her the world on a silver platter. Unfortunately she couldn't give her the one thing that would make her happy. Steven.

"Well, see you later." Cara gave a small wave. "I won't be back too late."

Her mother's brow creased. "Cara?" She got up again, went over to her daughter, and put a comforting arm around her. "Do me a favor and smile, dear. You know, if you pretend hard enough, you might wind up fooling yourself and having fun."

Cara gave her mother a hard hug. "I guess I don't have anything to lose by trying."

She kept her mother's advice in mind on the ride to Guido's and pasted a smile on her face as she pushed open the doors of the pizzeria. Her smile faded the split second she walked inside. There, at a booth near the artificial waterfall that cascaded down the rear wall, sat Steven and Ferney.

Ferney's bubbly giggle filled the air as surely

as the rich, pungent aroma of pizza. Steven was obviously enthralled. His eyes never left her face.

Cara waited just a moment too long before spinning around to try to make a quick exit. "Cara, over here," she heard Maria call out.

Steven heard Maria too. He whipped his head around and focused on Cara. His cheeks were pink with embarrassment, and he had the nervous look of someone caught cheating on a test. He gave a feeble wave.

Cara wished she could melt into the floor. Her body trembled, and she felt sick to her stomach. She stood there, rooted to the spot, paralyzed with misery.

"Uh, ah, would you like to join us, Cara?" Steven's flustered voice came to her as if through a fog. None of this seemed real. It was too terrible to be real.

Somehow she managed to move toward his table. Her legs were weak. "Steve, I *do* want to join you. You don't know how much I want to. But I don't think there's any room here for me." She allowed herself one last look at Steven's face, the face she loved. Then she turned and walked away stiffly, heading straight for the door.

"Cara!" Maria ran up to her. "Cara, where are you going? Stay here. Cara, you can't let some dumb guy chase you out of here. Cara, I'm talking to you. . . ."

Maria was still appealing to her as Cara left the

pizzeria. But Cara barely heard her through the pounding in her head. She raced to the parking lot and collapsed against the side of her car, warm, salty tears streaming down her cheeks. She had thought there were no more tears to cry, but she couldn't have been more wrong.

Only a few short days before, Cara had actually been excited about meeting Ferney. Now she wished with all her might that the girl had never set foot on California soil. Cara dabbed at her eyes with the edge of her shirt. This whole exchange program that Ms. Dalton had dreamed up was turning out to be a monumental disaster.

"To the best idea the French department ever had!" Jessica raised her glass in a toast.

Jean-Claude tapped the side of his glass against hers, producing a bell-like tinkle. "And to the most beautiful guest in Cannes."

"I'll drink to that!" Jessica took a few sips of champagne. "Mmm, this is delicious." Jean-Claude really knew how to do things with style.

After a perfect day spent basking in the sun, waterskiing and swimming and diving off his friend's boat, Jean-Claude had whisked Jessica off to a tiny restaurant in the mountains high above the city. They sat on an outdoor deck at a polished-wood table, champagne in an ice bucket, as the sun dropped low in the sky and began sinking into the ocean. The sky was a deep, purple-blue above, glowing stripes of pink and orange below.

"This is incredible!" Jessica said. As it grew darker, the lights of Cannes appeared, twinkling in the valley. The first star of the evening shone overhead. Jessica pointed to it. "Oh, look! You can make a wish on it, you know."

"I wish that as long as you are here, every day can be as wonderful as this one." Jean-Claude held his champagne glass up toward the star.

"No, you're not supposed to say it out loud, otherwise it won't come true," Jessica explained.

"Don't you believe it. We can make it happen if we want to." Jean-Claude stretched his arms across the small table and cupped Jessica's face in his large, strong hands. "Don't you think so?"

Jessica's answer was to lean forward and turn her face up toward his. His breath was warm as he gently lowered his mouth onto hers. She could taste the trace of salty ocean water mingled with champagne on his lips.

"Ah, Elizabeth," he murmured.

She pulled away abruptly. If only Jean-Claude would quit calling her Elizabeth. It was the one dark cloud in an otherwise flawless day. But she couldn't tell him the truth. Not now, at least. It was still too soon. She would have to wait until he was so much in love that he wouldn't care who she was.

"What's the matter?" Jean-Claude frowned. "Don't you want me to kiss you?"

Jessica focused on Jean-Claude's handsome face once more, melting in his amber-eyed gaze. She pressed her moist lips to his in a long, lingering kiss. They separated for a split second, then came together again for an even more passionate kiss.

"Does that answer your question?" Jessica whispered breathlessly.

"Ahem!" Behind her a waiter cleared his throat. *"Monsieur, mademoiselle, excusez-moi."* He placed a steaming tureen of bouillabaisse on the table, ladling out a portion for each of them.

Jessica breathed in the aroma. In the hearty broth were various different kinds of fish, langoustines—tiny French lobsters—clams, scallops, crabs, and several types of seafood that she couldn't identify. "Wow!" The American exclamation was the best way to put it.

Jean-Claude laughed. "I like this word. 'Wow!' " He imitated Jessica as closely as he could. "It sounds like its meaning. 'Wow!' "

"Not bad," Jessica complimented him. "What do you say in French?"

"Fantastique, incroyable, magnifique, superbe, splendide—"

"Whoa. Slow down!" Jessica held up her hands. "One at a time, *d'accord?"* She made Jean-Claude say the words again, and she repeated each one, trying to commit each to memory. Elizabeth would be proud of her, she thought.

Elizabeth. There was an irritating prick of guilt again as Jessica thought about her twin.

"Aren't you going to try it?" Jean-Claude's voice broke into her thoughts.

"What? Oh, the soup." Jessica took a mouthful of the bouillabaisse. A piece of soft, tender fish melted in her mouth. The broth was perfectly seasoned.

"Good?" asked Jean-Claude.

"Fantastique, incroyable, magnifique, superbe, splendide!" she joked. "In other words, wow!" Jessica summoned up all her enthusiasm and tried to push Elizabeth's image out of her mind.

For the most part it worked, thanks to the food, the champagne, the romantic setting, and Jean-Claude's handsome face and warm touch. But somewhere, in a tiny corner of her mind, a trace of misgiving had taken root so firmly that it continued to nag at her subtly throughout the evening.

Not enough, however, to stop her from accepting a date with Jean-Claude for the following day.

"Tennis tomorrow, the way we'd planned?" he asked as he pulled up to the Glizes' house at the end of the evening.

Jessica nodded.

"Good. I can't wait." He pulled her close to him, "It's been a marvelous day. I've enjoyed being with you so much. Even more than yesterday."

Guilt surfaced again in Jessica's heart. "Well, you know me better now," she said, trying to explain away the difference that Jean-Claude clearly sensed between her and her sister.

"Whatever." Jean-Claude wrapped his powerful arms around her and kissed her forehead, her eyes, the tip of her nose, and finally her lips, his mouth urgently seeking hers.

Jessica yearned to abandon herself to his embrace, but she didn't dare. It was too dangerous to let him park in front of the house for too long. If Elizabeth saw them, it would be all over. "Jean-Claude, I'd better go in now."

"I'll pick you up here at one," Jean-Claude proposed, still holding Jessica tightly.

"Umm, maybe it would be better if I met you at your grandmother's house," Jessica said. Under no circumstances did she want Jean-Claude knocking on the door the next day. She would have to figure out where the countess lived, but she imagined that everyone in the area must know.

"Fine. I'm sure Grandmother will be delighted to see you again," Jean-Claude said. "She really liked you."

Jessica looked down at the dashboard. "Yes, I, ah, felt the same way about her." *Whoever she is*, she added silently, the fingers of her right hand crossed behind her back.

"So I'll see you there tomorrow," Jean-Claude

confirmed. He and Jessica came together for one final embrace.

"Jess? Is that you?" Elizabeth's voice caught up with Jessica as she was sneaking up the staircase to the bedroom. "Hello? Jessica?"

It looked as though Jessica was going to have to face her twin. She turned and slowly headed back downstairs.

"Hi, Liz," she said, sitting down next to her on the couch and trying like mad to ignore her conscience, as well as the unhappy expression on Liz's face.

"Hi, Jess. How was your day?" Elizabeth's attempt to sound cheerful failed miserably.

Jessica felt even worse. A voice inside her was pushing her, telling her to level with her sister, to come clean and admit what she'd done. Elizabeth was so forgiving. It wouldn't be that difficult. She fiddled with the strap of her beach bag, figuring out how to explain the whole situation to her twin.

"Liz?" She summoned up her courage.

"Yes, Jessica?"

But she couldn't. Even if Elizabeth did understand, she would probably insist that Jessica tell Jean-Claude the truth immediately. If there was one thing Elizabeth couldn't tolerate, it was a lie. Then Jean-Claude might decide that Jessica wasn't worth spending his time with. No, she couldn't risk it. Jean-Claude was too terrific. There was no way she was going to jeopardize what they had going.

"Liz, um, ah, my day was fine. How was yours?"

"Oh, Jessica, everything got all messed up," Elizabeth said.

Jessica shifted uncomfortably on the couch, avoiding her twin's eye. "What happened?"

"Well, I was supposed to see Jean-Claude today, but right after you left, Avery called." Bit by bit, the story tumbled out—the wait in the pharmacy, the car accident, and finally Elizabeth's phone call to Jean-Claude. "It's funny that he didn't call me back," she finished. "Do you think he'd be that mad at me for missing our date?"

Jessica's attention was riveted to one spot on the tile floor. "It doesn't really matter that much, does it? I mean you weren't that crazy about the guy in the first place, right?" She didn't dare look at Elizabeth's face.

"I just met him," Elizabeth answered. "But he did seem very nice."

"But not sensational," Jessica prodded, growing a bit bolder.

"Well, it was kind of hard to tell. We only spent a few hours together."

A few hours? Jessica had been able to tell in a few seconds what a special person Jean-Claude was. After a few hours, she was absolutely, positively head-over-heels in love! It just went to show that it was supposed to happen this way. He and Jessica were fated to meet. She pushed harder.

"Liz, what you're saying is that you weren't knocked out. It wasn't love at first sight."

"No, I can't say it was. But why are you quizzing me like this?"

Jessica ignored her sister's question and continued on her own track. "I mean you didn't find him all that marvelous or fabulous. It wasn't like you *had* to be with him." She was describing her own feelings for Jean-Claude.

"I guess not," Elizabeth said, but any further response was cut short by the ringing of the telephone. "Speak of the devil, maybe that's him now." She started to get up from the couch.

Jessica was out of her seat in a flash. "Don't bother, Liz, I'll get it." She raced past her twin, dashing into the kitchen to pick up the receiver. "Allô?" she said.

Sure enough, Jean-Claude's voice came over the line. "Elizabeth?" he asked.

"Yes," Jessica responded. She glanced back and saw a vague look of disappointment flit across her sister's face. *Well, she'll get over it*, Jessica thought. After all, Elizabeth had said herself that she wasn't in love with Jean-Claude. Jessica, on the other hand, was thrilled just to hear his voice.

"It's Jean-Claude," he was saying.

"I know," she answered. "Do you miss me already?" she added jokingly.

"Actually, I do. But I'm telephoning for another reason. Our housekeeper said you called here and left some sort of message apologizing for not being at home this afternoon. I don't understand."

Jessica lowered her voice so that Elizabeth wouldn't hear her. "Neither do I, Jean-Claude. I never called there. How could I? I was out with you all day."

There was silence on the other end. "I can't figure it out. I guess Jacqueline got the message wrong."

"I guess."

"OK, so I'll see you tomorrow. Good night, Elizabeth."

"Good night, Jean-Claude," Jessica said. She hung up and went back to the living room.

Elizabeth was thumbing through a copy of *Elle*, the French version of *Mademoiselle*. She looked up as Jessica came in. "Marc?" she asked.

"Mmm." Jessica nodded, but didn't exactly say yes.

"Oh." Elizabeth's tone was flat. "Well, I guess I'm not going to hear from Jean-Claude. That really surprises me. I thought he was more polite than that."

"So maybe he's not worth thinking about anymore," Jessica suggested. Once her twin got Jean-Claude out of her mind altogether, Jessica could extinguish that last flicker of guilt she felt and enjoy being with him without reservation.

"You're right, Jess. I promise to try not to lose any sleep over him."

Jessica grinned. "That's what I like to hear."

It was the last word either of them said concerning Jean-Claude that night.

Eleven

The morning sun flooded the balcony. The air was sweet, and the birds sang in the trees that blanketed the hills. It was a glorious day. But Elizabeth would have enjoyed it more if she weren't feeling so lonely. Cannes stretched out before her, but she had no one to share it with.

She allowed herself to pretend that she was with Todd again, that he had never moved away, and that he'd come on the exchange program with her. She pictured them sitting at a café over coffee, strolling along the bay at sunset, visiting the sights hand in hand.

It was the first time she had let her imagination loose like this in a very long time. It wasn't that she really wanted Todd to be there with her. It

was just that she wanted so badly to have somebody, anybody, with whom she could share the
beauty of this place and the adventure of a foreign country.

Jessica was off with her new friend again, and
René couldn't have made it clearer that he
wanted to have nothing to do with her. Elizabeth
looked over the balcony at him as he lay on the
lawn, looking at the newspaper. In a way, they
actually had a number of things in common. He
was well read, he jogged every morning, he
seemed to enjoy quiet moments by himself. But
she couldn't overcome the grudge he bore
against her. It wasn't fair.

And then just when she thought she'd made a
friend, Jean-Claude had given up on her because
she'd been a little late to meet him. What was the
matter with these French boys anyway?

A hard laugh escaped Elizabeth. She was
beginning to think like René. It had nothing to
do with him or Jean-Claude being French. She
had simply had some bad luck so far. She
couldn't let it make her bitter or spoil her
vacation. There were plenty of things she could
do by herself. Especially now that she knew how
to get to the center of Cannes by bus.

She would get a table at the Festival and write.
She had always harbored a secret dream about
being a writer in France. So many great novelists
had worked there. She would have lunch at one
of the little waterside restaurants. And in the

afternoon she would finally lie on the beach and swim in the Mediterranean. There was no reason to depend on someone else for that.

It was going to be a good day after all, Elizabeth told herself resolutely. She went inside to get ready. René could sit on the lawn until he turned into a plant, and Jean-Claude—well, as Jessica had pointed out the night before, he wasn't worth sweating about. Wherever he was.

"Hi, Jean-Claude." Jessica stood at the doorstep of the countess's house in her white tennis shirt and skirt, edged with pale blue. "All ready?" She swung her racket, feeling pleased with herself for finding the mansion so easily. The first person she had talked to in the neighborhood had been able to point her in the right direction.

"It's impossible to miss," he had said.

He hadn't been kidding, Jessica thought. It was one of the most magnificent houses she had ever seen. Bigger than Lila Fowler's or Bruce Patman's, grander and more beautiful than both of them put together. The perfectly tended estate grounds took Jessica's breath away.

But she had forgotten about the mansion and gardens the second Jean-Claude had opened the door. Now he wrapped his arms around her and kissed her hard on the mouth. "All ready," he said. He picked up his own tennis racket from the hallway and dropped the car keys into his shorts pocket.

"Oh, by the way, Grandmother had to be at some meeting about next year's film festival, but she asked me to tell you she was sorry she missed you and she hopes you'll come back soon and pay her a visit."

"Oh, um, of course." Jessica was relieved that the old lady wasn't home. Chatting it up with adults was more Elizabeth's style than hers. But if Jean-Claude thought she and his grandmother were friends, she would play it that way. "Tell her I'm sorry I missed her."

"Sure, but I must admit that personally, I'm not sorry she's out. It gives me more time to spend with you." Jean-Claude brushed Jessica's cheek with his fingertips.

Jessica tingled at his touch. It felt so right, being with Jean-Claude. There was a special magic in the simple gesture of his fingers caressing her face. She covered his hand with her own.

Then, on tiptoe, she leaned forward, and they kissed again, their mouths pressing together hungrily. When their lips parted, Jean-Claude looked deep into her eyes and gave her a warm, intimate smile. This was going to be another magnificent day, Jessica thought.

Later in the day, Elizabeth headed up the hill

from where the bus had dropped her off. Much to her surprise, it had been a nice day. All it had taken was the determination to get out and do things on her own. Not that she wouldn't have enjoyed the company of a friend, but there was a certain challenge in getting around by herself, and she had risen to the occasion. She was proud of herself.

In the morning she had wandered around the harbor, watching fishermen at work and looking in wonder at the magnificent yachts, some of which seemed as big as or bigger than her house in Sweet Valley. On the deck of one of the largest, a woman in nothing but a bikini and piles of gold jewelry had been entertaining friends, seemingly immune to the stares of the numerous passersby.

On the other side of the docks, a mime was working the crowd of tourists. Elizabeth had watched a few minutes, deposited a one-franc coin in the hat he passed around, and then strolled over to the nearby flower market. There she had talked to some of the vendors, learning the French names for a whole spectrum of flowers and plants. Later, she wrote postcards to all her friends back home over coffee at the Festival and added a new entry to her diary. After a superb lunch, she had stretched out on the white sand for an afternoon of beaching and swimming.

Now she gave a few skips as the Glizes' house

came into view. Her skin was warm and tingling from the sun. She whistled to herself. As she approached the edge of the front lawn, she peered into the mailbox. Perhaps it was a bit too soon for a letter to have arrived from home, but if her parents had written immediately, there might be something in there for her and Jessica.

She reached to the back of the box and felt something. She pulled it out. An airmail envelope. Great! She turned it over, expecting to see her father's elaborate, round handwriting or her mother's broad scrawl. It was neither of those. The letter was addressed to René. There was no return address, but it was postmarked Boston. Maybe it was from his father. René would certainly want to see this right away.

Elizabeth rushed inside. "René?" she called out.

"Yes? What is it?" His voice came from the kitchen.

She found him sitting at the table, snacking on a piece of apple tart left over from the other night. "This arrived for you." She placed the envelope in front of him.

René glanced at it, then scowled. He picked it up and deposited it in the trash can.

"Aren't you even going to read it?"

"No. He made enough of a statement by leaving us in the first place. I haven't read one of his letters yet, and I don't intend to." René picked up his knife and fork, cut a large piece of tart, and continued eating. He clearly considered this the end of the discussion.

Elizabeth sank down on one of the kitchen chairs. "That's all you have to say about it?"

René put down his fork and swiveled around to face her. "It's really none of your business, but if you must know, he writes to me every month. And every month I throw the letter out unopened." Rene's tone was flat.

Elizabeth thought his calmness was even worse than if he had been yelling and screaming. He was making too great an effort to hold back his emotions, an effort he had probably been making every month for years.

Every month! Elizabeth thought. She had imagined René's father as a cold, uncaring man who had abandoned his family with never another word or attempt to contact them. But a man who took the time to write to his son every single month couldn't be one-hundred-percent horrible. There had to be two sides to this story. She realized that so far René's was the only one she'd heard.

"René, your father writes every single month, and you never read even one single sentence? How do you know you're not being unfair to him?" She studied René's strong-jawed, handsome face. It remained immobile.

"I just know," he answered, like a stubborn child.

"How?" she probed.

The wall that hid his feelings began crumbling. "Look, you've done nothing but cause trouble for me since you got here. I wish you'd never come." René slammed his hand down on the table. "Just having you around all the time is bad enough, but when you start butting into my private life, that's where I draw the line!" His shouting reverberated off the walls. "You Americans have got to be the rudest people in the world, poking around in things that don't concern you!"

Elizabeth took a few deep breaths. She had lost her temper with René several times already, and it hadn't helped matters. Staying calm was the key if she was ever going to get through his shell of hurt and anger.

"René, what are you so afraid of finding out by opening that letter? That maybe you haven't been entirely right about your father?" She spoke gently but insistently.

"I'm sure I'm right. So why bother opening it?" René turned back to the table and attacked the rest of his apple tart, polishing it off in a few bites.

"If you're so sure, then what do you have to lose by opening it?" Elizabeth challenged him.

René opened his mouth and abruptly closed it again, as if he didn't have an answer.

"Go ahead," she said softly, taking the letter out of the trash and placing it in front of him.

It was a gamble. Elizabeth didn't know for certain that the contents of the envelope were worth reading, but at a rate of one letter per month, it was a gamble she felt fairly safe taking. René's father undoubtedly had his faults, but if he put this much time and energy into reaching out to his son, he couldn't be as much of an ogre as René seemed to think.

"And what if I don't open it? I suppose you're going to do it for me?"

"No. I know you think I'm like that, the kind of person to meddle in other people's business, but that's not true. I wish I could make you understand that." Elizabeth spoke firmly, but there was an appeal in her voice.

"And forcing me to read something I don't want to read is going to help?" René asked sarcastically.

"Maybe."

"Well, tough. I'm not laying a finger on that envelope. What are you going to do about that?"

Elizabeth decided to give it to him straight. Maybe it wouldn't work, but nothing else had, either. "René, listen to yourself. Whenever the subject of your father comes up, you sound like an angry little boy. It's not you talking, at least not the René who's eighteen. It's the child whose father left him and hurt him so horribly. An adult would read that letter, whether he thought he would like what it said or not. You have to deal with it. You can't turn away forever."

Elizabeth's words had broken through to

René. He said nothing, but he seemed to be listening to her, to be thinking about what she was saying.

She encouraged him. "Come on. Don't keep burying what you feel."

René remained poker-faced, yet he reached one hand slowly forward.

At that precise instant, Jessica waltzed into the kitchen, sun burnished and still wet from what looked like a late-day swim. "Hi, Liz," she sang out. She didn't bother greeting René.

Elizabeth's heart sank. What a moment for her twin to show up! Just when it appeared that she had reached René. "Hi, Jessica," she said guardedly. She hoped her sister would catch her tone and get the message to leave the room.

But Jessica went blithely to the refrigerator, selected a container of pear yogurt, and grabbed a spoon, making herself comfortable on one of the chairs. "Boy, what a great day!" she exclaimed, peeling back the foil top on the yogurt container. "Really incredible!"

"Oh?" Maybe if she let Jessica talk, she'd describe her day, finish her snack, and then leave her and René by themselves again.

"Do you know what it's like to swim in the Mediterrean?" Jessica gave a satisfied sigh. "Well, it's great."

"Sounds nice," Elizabeth managed, but she was only listening with one ear. Most of her concentration was still on René. Reading that letter from his father would be such an important step for him. She hated to see this moment shattered.

"It was better than nice," Jessica said. "Of course, René here wouldn't understand. I mean the big, brave guy is so afraid of a little water that he hasn't been near it in years. Isn't that so?" She flashed René a nasty smile.

Elizabeth was horrified. "Jess, how could you?" She glared at her sister. She hadn't told her twin René's painful story so that she could use it as ammunition against him. He hadn't been a gracious host, but Jessica's remark was inexcusable, and her timing couldn't have been worse.

René's face grew hard. "Who told you about that?" he demanded.

"Liz," Jessica said matter-of-factly.

Elizabeth wished the floor would open up and swallow her. She saw René's green eyes blaze, silently accusing her of being a meddling busybody and a malicious gossip. He didn't have to say it aloud. Perhaps he had begun to soften toward her before Jessica had walked in, but now he was right back to thinking every bad thing he'd ever thought about her, and then some.

He snatched the letter from his father and held it high in the air. "As I said, I don't need to open it. You people are all made from the same despicable mold." He whipped the envelope into the wastebasket again and stormed out of the room.

153

Elizabeth slumped down on the kitchen table, her head in her hands. "Jessica Wakefield, I can't believe what you just did to him."

"What do you mean? I gave him exactly what he deserved! I've been waiting for a chance to get back at him ever since he started with us on the way home from the airport," Jessica said with an air of triumph. "And now I have. Did you see the expression on his face?"

Elizabeth shot her twin a look of white hot fire.

Jessica wasn't daunted. "You know, Liz, he's been even worse to you than to me. You should be thanking me for what I did." She stared back at Elizabeth. "By the way, what's this letter all about?" She got up and reached into the trash can.

Elizabeth jumped up and yanked it out of her hands. "Jessica, it's not your concern."

"Oh, come on, Liz."

"No." There was finality in her tone.

Jessica's eyes narrowed. "I don't know what's wrong with you. I come in here in a great mood, and you do your very best to bring me down as low as you can. Well, let me tell you something. It worked." She stormed out of the kitchen.

A second later she was back. "And P.S. Don't expect me to be on your side next time René starts bugging you. If you're going to stick up for a jerk like that, you're welcome to him." Jessica made another dramatic exit. This time for real.

Elizabeth stared down at the envelope in her

hands, more concerned about that than about her sister's performance. She had come so close with René. But "almost" didn't count. In fact, in this case, it had turned out to be worse than if she hadn't tried at all.

Twelve

"David, this is Ferney. Ferney, my friend David. He's visiting for a couple of days." Steven Wakefield made the introductions. "David's a French major at my school," he continued. "I thought maybe he could help us out. You know, practice his translation skills."

Of course Ferney didn't understand a word. David stepped forward and shook her hand, simultaneously telling her what Steven had just said.

"Ah, *très bien.*" She giggled. *"Je suis très contente."*

"She says she's really glad," David said. Then he shook his head. "Boy, I don't know how the two of you have managed to communicate a single thing to each other so far."

Steven laughed. "It's been easier than you think. It's all in the chemistry between us." He smiled at Ferney, noticing the way she had pulled her strawberry-blond curls back into an off-center ponytail. Very French, he thought. She smiled back.

"Steve, she's very attractive. I'll admit that. But chemistry isn't a language. How do you know what she's really like? Or she you, for that matter?"

"We have our ways. Like I know she wants to be a scientist. Why don't you ask her about that?" Steven suggested.

"Sure." David turned to Ferney and started talking. She replied. David said something else.

Steven followed the sound of their voices without understanding the first thing that they were saying. But he didn't miss the tiny frown that appeared on David's face.

"What is it?" he asked.

"It seems you weren't exactly right. Science is her favorite subject in school, it's true. But she says she has no intention of actually becoming a scientist. She just likes experimenting in the lab, watching chemicals turn different colors, figuring out the amounts of calories in various foods, looking at things under microscopes. She says it's more fun than sitting at a desk and listening to a teacher drone on and on. She told me about some experiment she did to make a new lipstick color. Do you want to hear about it?"

Steven felt a sense of disappointment wash over him. "Um, no. No, thanks." He thought about Tricia's noble aspirations, all the ways she used to talk about putting science to good use. Oh, well. He tried to throw off his disillusionment. He couldn't expect Ferney and Tricia to be exactly the same.

Steven shrugged. "To each her own," he commented to David. "Why don't you ask her how she likes Sweet Valley?"

Again he waited while David and Ferney conversed.

"She says she's having fun," David reported. "She made a date with some of the other French kids on the exchange program for lunch tomorrow. They're going to that new crepe place over in Estrella Beach."

"Crepes? Doesn't she want to try something she can't have in France?" Steven asked.

David translated. Ferney giggled and said something in French. "She likes crepes," David explained.

"Oh." Steven was feeling more and more deflated. He kept anticipating Tricia's wit, intelligence, and maturity in Ferney's answers, and he was getting none of that. Perhaps he was asking the wrong questions. Maybe if he asked her about the book he'd seen her reading the other night, he could steer the discussion in a more interesting direction. She had been poring over a copy of *The Bald Soprano,* a play by the renowned French playwright Ionesco. Steven had read a translation of it in his modern drama class in college the previous semester, and loved it.

"David, Ferney's reading *The Bald Soprano,*" Steven said.

"Oh, Ionesco? He's great, isn't he?" David remarked. "*The Bald Soprano*'s really funny." He turned to Ferney and began talking again. As she replied, Steven saw him frown once more.

"She's only reading it because it's a homework assignment," David said. "She prefers fashion magazines."

There was a pregnant silence in the Wakefield living room. Steven was afraid to have David ask Ferney another question. Her answers were not at all what he had expected to hear. Suddenly he clapped his hands. "Hey, what do you say we all change into our bathing suits and go for a swim in the pool?" He and Ferney had done just fine without talking. Perhaps it was a mistake to do too much of it all at once.

David seemed relieved. "That sounds great to me. Ferney? *On va nager?*"

She nodded, pleased with the suggestion.

"Good," said Steven. "What are we waiting for?" His voice was cheerful, but inside, a seed of doubt about Ferney was sprouting. Perhaps the problem was simply due to the awkwardness of trying to communicate through David's translations. It wasn't the most natural way to have a discussion. But for the first time since her arrival, Steven was opening his eyes to the fact that there might be truth to what his parents had been trying to tell him all along. Perhaps the Ferney who had captured his imagination was someone he had largely made up in his mind. And now that David was here, he was going to have to get to know the *real* Ferney.

Steven had thought that inviting his friend down for a few days was a terrific idea, that it would help bring him and Ferney closer. Suddenly he wasn't entirely sure he'd been right.

Avery Glize had been wrong about something, too, and she was apologizing to Elizabeth for it.

"I feel just terrible that René has been so uncordial to you. You know, it seemed that he was finally getting over his negative feelings about Americans, and I thought having you two here would be a last step. I imagined he might really enjoy your company." Avery shook her head. "It didn't occur to me that it would be a giant step backward for him or that he would make you so unhappy." The corners of her mouth turned down.

Elizabeth hadn't planned to tell Avery about the incident with René. Apparently, however, René had made some cryptic remark to his mother that made her suspect something unpleasant had happened. She had taken Elizabeth aside after dinner to ask her about it, and Elizabeth had wound up giving her what she hoped was an unbiased version of what had taken place a few hours earlier.

Avery couldn't apologize enough. "I hope you'll forgive me, Elizabeth. I did so want you to have a wonderful time here in Cannes," she said. "I feel just terrible about all this. I should have realized—I should have been able to see what would happen."

"Please don't blame yourself. I know you wanted only the best for everyone. And don't worry about me. Really. Most of my day was great!" Elizabeth reassured her. "I just hope I didn't make René hurt any worse than he already did. I guess I never should have encouraged him to read that letter."

"Elizabeth, you did what I've done hundreds of times. I beg René to give his father a chance every time one of those airmail letters arrives." Avery sank down on the love seat in the foyer, where they had gone to talk privately.

"Gordon, René's father, did an irresponsible, unforgivable thing when he left his children. I'm the last person to deny that. But it wasn't entirely his fault. We were so young when we met, and so impulsive," she confided to Elizabeth. "We were married and had two infants almost before we knew it. We rushed into

162

something that we ought to have considered beforehand with the utmost seriousness. But we didn't know. We were children ourselves. Not much older than you or René are now." Her eyes were moist. "It was too much pressure. Neither of us could cope. We began fighting, taking it out on each other. In the end I think we both felt that anything was better than that."

"So your husband just—he just left?" Elizabeth felt close to tears herself.

Avery nodded. "I swore I'd never have anything to do with him again and that he would never, ever get near my children. I thought he didn't deserve their love." She paused. "Gordon had a few wild years after he left us. But, Elizabeth, people grow up. They change. He settled down a long time ago and became the caring human being who had been buried deep inside him when we were married. I suppose I always sensed that side of him, or I never would have gotten involved with him to begin with. But that part of his nature blossomed too late for me."

Avery was quiet for a few moments, lost in reflection. "But I've gotten away from my original point," she said. "Which is that it's too late for Gordon and me, but not for him and his children. Oh, I was vehemently opposed to any kind of reunion for a very long time, but when he began writing to us so regularly and his letters were so warm and tender, I realized that I was depriving my children of their father's love. He was trying too hard for me to keep holding a grudge that only caused more hurt to all of us."

Avery's voice was shaky. "But by then, I had conveyed so much of my hatred and anger to René that he was unable even to consider any contact with his father. Ferney was too young to remember the pain of Gordon's departure, so it was easier for her. They correspond quite frequently now and take vacations together. You know, she's going to stop off and visit him in Cambridge on her way back from Sweet Valley."

"No, I didn't know," Elizabeth said softly.

"Yes. Gordon and the woman he married have a baby girl. My children's half-sister. Their father wants so much for all of them to be real family to each other. He won't give up on René. They were so close before Gordon left. He's written him hundreds of letters and postcards. His wife has written, too. She seems like a lovely woman. But René is so stubborn he won't look at a single word."

"It's understandable," Elizabeth remarked gently. "In order to do that, he has to face the hurt of what happened all over again."

"That's true, of course. Elizabeth, you're a very perceptive, sensitive young woman. My son ought to be happy to have you as a guest in our house." Avery patted her arm. "You're a good listener, too. If anyone should be able to prove to René that his impressions of Americans are false, it's you."

164

"I wish I could. I wanted so badly for René and me to be friends, but it won't work. He's set on disliking me. Most of the time, he won't even look at me, and when he does, it's even worse. He just glares at me."

"Oh, Elizabeth, don't give up. My son has been deeply wounded by his father. He's furious, confused, and bitter when he thinks about what happened. But he's a wonderful boy in so many other ways. If only he would open up to you, you'd see that."

Elizabeth nodded. "I have seen it, I think, for brief moments when he's let down his guard or when he doesn't know I'm watching him. But I guess I remind him too much of what he doesn't want to think about. Avery, he'll be better off when my vacation here is over."

"Perhaps," Avery said sadly.

There was little else to say. René made no effort to conceal the fact that his father was the enemy. And by virtue of the nationality they shared, Elizabeth and Jessica were the enemy, too. It wasn't rational, but passionate emotions never were. They could sweep a person along a path that was beyond his or her control, like a twig in a rushing river.

Avery got up and pulled herself together. "Well, thank goodness that at least one of my children has her father back," she murmured, more to herself than to Elizabeth. "I ought to be grateful for that. I ought to be grateful about Ferney."

Elizabeth nodded. But thoughts of Ferney did not console her the way they did Avery. In fact, Ferney was just one more thing for Elizabeth to worry about. She looked too much like Tricia Martin to leave Steven's heart unstirred. Elizabeth wondered if the French girl's presence was causing as many problems in Sweet Valley as hers and Jessica's were in Cannes. She hoped and prayed that was not the case.

"I feel like such a fool," Steven said, toying with the straw in his thick chocolate shake. "I was so busy noticing how she looked that I was blind to her in every other way." He sat opposite David at a side booth at the Dairi Burger.

"Steve, it could happen to anyone. Tricia was such an important part of your life. It's understandable that you'd react the way you did," David responded. "Besides, you're opening your eyes to the truth now. That's what's important."

"Thanks to you," Steven said. "If you hadn't been here to tell me what she was saying, I might have gone through the rest of her stay here fooling myself into believing she was somebody she wasn't. It's amazing. Just one day of actually being able to communicate with her, and I find out that, well, I guess Ferney is very young. Not that deep. I mean, I figure she'll grow up to be a nice enough person, but right now she's, ah, sort of, you know, silly." He searched for a tactful way of expressing what had been obvious to everyone but him.

"You mean she's not your emotional equal?" David supplied helpfully.

"Yeah. Exactly. Not the way Tricia was." Steven lowered his voice. "Or Cara is." There! He had said it out loud. That was what was really bothering him. In all of this, Cara was the one who had gotten hurt. He had been too wrapped up in his own feelings to consider hers.

"You know, David," he continued, "when I first met Cara, she was more like Ferney is now, more into her own personal pleasures, less aware of people around her, less adult, I guess. But she's come a long way. Her soul—it's more like Tricia's, even though she might not look like her. Besides, she's got her own beauty."

He paused, picturing Cara's face. "God, she's beautiful," he whispered. "And she's a very special person."

"Steve, you have to tell her that she's the one you really want," David said.

Steven took a sip of his shake. "If she'll have me. After what I've done, I wouldn't blame her if she never wanted to speak to me again." He remembered her expression at Guido's when she'd seen him with Ferney. It wasn't a look of anger so much as one of searing pain. She didn't deserve it. If anyone should be going through that kind of agony, it was Steven himself. He was responsible. "David, I'm so disgusted with myself. I've been a selfish, spoiled child at Cara's expense."

"Steve, you can't remedy anything by berating yourself. Going to Cara and explaining how you really feel is the only thing to do."

Steven nodded. "You're right. She might never forgive me, but I've got to try. Heck, at this point, I don't have a thing to lose, do I?"

Thirteen

It was the midpoint of Elizabeth's vacation in Cannes. She was alone, out on her balcony, reading, when she heard the faint ringing of the door bell. Marking her place, she closed the book and ran downstairs to pull open the heavy wooden door.

A short boy with frizzy, brown hair stood on the doorstep. "Jessica, I apologize for bothering you," he said in halting English, "but I wanted to know if you're feeling better."

"No, I'm not Jessica," Elizabeth responded in French. "I'm Elizabeth, her twin sister."

"Ah, yes, she told me about you," the boy said, speaking more easily in his native language. "Nice to meet you. My name is Marc." He extended his hand.

Elizabeth shook it. "Nice to meet you, too, but I'm afraid I don't understand." Her brow wrinkled. "I thought Jessica was with you today."

"You are saying she is not here?" Marc looked concerned. "But she is all right?" he asked.

"She was fine when she left here a little while ago. I thought she was going to play tennis with you. You did call last night to make plans, didn't you?"

Marc shook his head. "Perhaps it was somebody else," he mused sadly, hurt coloring his face.

Elizabeth experienced an unpleasant shiver up and down her arms—the kind she felt whenever her twin was up to one of her tricks. Jessica hadn't actually told her it was Marc she was meeting for tennis, but she had a way of implying something that was almost as good as saying it. Now, however, it was clear to Elizabeth that Jessica had found somebody more to her liking, and that she had simply dropped Marc.

Elizabeth had harbored a suspicion that something like this would happen from the day Jessica had told her about Marc. In fact, she even remembered pleading with her sister to be nice to the poor guy. But Jessica, as usual, had done exactly as she pleased. And behind Elizabeth's

170

back, too, so she wouldn't have to admit what she'd done.

Elizabeth felt sympathy for Marc welling up inside of her. One glance and it was obvious that he could never be Jessica's type in a million years. Yet here he was, coming to see how she was. Darn Jessica! This was just so unfair.

Marc stood with his head down, shifting uncomfortably from one foot to the other. "I wanted to see if Jessica would come to the opening of an art exhibit with me this afternoon. My parents got an invitation, but they couldn't go, so I thought Jessica and I—" He paused. "But I guess that's impossible." He looked up at Elizabeth shyly. "I don't suppose that—no, never mind." He waved his hand. "Well, I'll leave you alone. I'm sorry to have disturbed you."

Elizabeth took in Marc's miserable expression. He looked so lonely. For an instant she identified with him completely. True, she had enjoyed her day alone yesterday, but so many days of solitude in a row were not exactly what she had in mind for this trip. On impulse, she put her hand out to stop Marc from going. It was obvious that he had been about to invite her to go along with him, but since he was shy, she knew it was up to her to take the initiative.

"Marc, I love art exhibits," Elizabeth said. In fact, they were much more her style than her sister's anyway, though she didn't say that to Marc.

It would only drive home the fact that he and Jessica were as mismatched as a flower-print dress and argyle socks. Instead, she simply told him, "I know I'm not Jessica, but if you want some company, I'd be happy to go with you."

Marc brightened visibly. "That would be very nice," he said.

"Great! Do you mind waiting a few minutes while I get ready?" Elizabeth asked.

"Of course not."

Five minutes later, Elizabeth came down the staircase in a crisp, off-white cotton dress, cut full with a V-neck front and back. She had added a scarf and a wristful of colorful bangles.

"You look very nice," Marc told her, his cheeks growing pink.

"Thank you."

Marc seemed very sweet, ever the gentleman, and although Elizabeth didn't feel any tingle of romance, she was pleased at the prospect of an afternoon with him. An art opening in Cannes conjured up all sorts of glamorous images in her mind. It was going to be fun.

Just as she and Marc were about to get into his car, René came screeching up on his moped. Elizabeth felt her anticipation give way to sick apprehension. René had skipped dinner the previous night, so she hadn't seen him since he'd raced from the kitchen after their fight. As René spotted her, tension swelled in the warm air.

"Hi, René," Elizabeth ventured timidly, halfway into Marc's silver Porsche. Marc, who had just gotten into the car, echoed her greeting, poking his head out the window.

"Hello, Marc." René was cordial enough to him. "And Jessica—why, no, it's Elizabeth." His cynical tone made it clear that it was a calculated slip. The disdain on his face was mixed with something she couldn't quite put her finger on. He came right up to her so that his remarks were audible to her alone. "All dressed up to steal your sister's boyfriend?" Contempt dripped from his words.

"He's not her boyfriend," Elizabeth whispered fiercely, trying to prevent Marc from over-hearing. "In fact, it seems to me that Jessica's trying to—"

No! Elizabeth snapped her mouth shut. What was she doing? She had started to explain that Jessica appeared to be trying to get rid of Marc. It began slipping out as she defended herself. But that was one piece of information she didn't want René to have. To confide in him would be disloyal to her twin. If it meant that René thought the worse of her, it couldn't be helped.

She got into the seat of Marc's car. "Goodbye, René." She shut her door. It was the only sensible thing to do. Arguing with him could only make the situation worse. Marc, unaware of the ugly words that had passed between Elizabeth and René, started the car and backed out of the driveway.

Elizabeth looked out the rear window at René. He stood openmouthed, as if ready to make another barbed comment. But there was no one to address it to. For a moment, she almost felt sorry for him. Perhaps she had been too hard on him. Jessica *had* been the one spending time with Marc, after all.

But Elizabeth couldn't ignore the way René had accused her. There was no excuse for that. She turned around in her seat. The only way to handle the situation with René was to avoid him as much as possible. Every time she tried to break through his shell, she only wound up making an even bigger mess of their relationship—if you could call less than a week of continual dispute a relationship. She was better off keeping her distance. There was no other solution.

"Mmmmm. I don't ever want to go back," Jessica murmured, gazing languidly at the scenery around her. The Ile Sainte-Marguerite, off the coast of Cannes, was one of the most beautiful places she had ever seen. The fragrance of the pine and eucalyptus trees that covered the island mingled with the fresh, salty smell of the sea. Artesian springs fed the large pond on one end of the island near where Jessica and Jean-Claude had docked the small boat on which they'd sailed over. Wild pheasants ran loose through the woods, and almond trees blossomed along the shore.

Jean-Claude had told her that there was a legend about those flowering trees. He explained that Saint Marguerite, for whom the island was named, was the sister of Saint Honorat, patron saint of a neighboring island. Ile Saint-Honorat loomed out of the Mediterranean, a bit farther out to sea than Sainte-Marguerite. According to the myth, Marguerite ran a nunnery on her island, while her brother followed his own religious rituals on his. Women were forbidden on Ile Saint-Honorat, so Marguerite had to wait for her brother to come to her for a visit. But Honorat was so caught up in religious duties that he would come only once a year, at the blossoming of the almond trees. Sorrowful because of the infrequency of his visits, Marguerite prayed so hard that an almond tree planted on the banks of her island burst into bloom and forever after remained that way.

Another story Jean-Claude told Jessica involved the fort on the island. In the distance, Jessica could see its massive walls. The fort had been built toward the end of the Middle Ages and used as a prison during the Renaissance. During that period it housed its most famous prisoner, nicknamed the Iron Mask because he never took off the mask that hid his face. His identity was concealed from the world, but some speculated that he was the adulterous brother of

Louis XIV, while others claimed he was a duke's secretary who had impersonated the king. Still others said he had helped poison one of the king's favorites at court. Another version of the Iron Mask story told of a doctor who had performed the autopsy on Louis XIII and questioned that the Sun King was his son and the true heir to the throne. It was for possession of such scandalous information that the doctor was imprisoned. He, said some, was the Iron Mask. The mysterious prisoner died without ever revealing who he was, perhaps more famous in his anonymity than he would have been had his identity been known.

Jessica was intrigued by all that Jean-Claude related to her. Iron Mask sounded like a character out of some novel about superheros and villains, and the setting of a centuries-old fort enhanced this thought.

It was so romantic, Jessica thought, being on an island whose physical beauty was matched by its legends and history. And, of course, even more romantic was the fact that Jean-Claude was next to her, stretched out on the blanket they had brought along with a picnic of freshly baked bread, several kinds of cheese, various salads, and a bottle of wine.

Jessica's head swam dizzily as she caressed his bare back, which was bronzed and warm from a day in the sun. She felt as if she might burst with happiness. "I want to stay here forever," she repeated to Jean-Claude.

Jean-Claude turned and kissed her forehead. *"Moi aussi*. I do too." He kissed her again. "But it looks as if the weather might be turning." He gestured at the sky. The sun, which had been shining all day, now flirted with clouds that grew denser and darker with every passing moment. "I want to be home before the sea starts getting too choppy," he said. "A little boat like that isn't made for rough water."

Jessica looked over at the sailboat. It wasn't much larger than a rowboat with a sail. Already it rocked from side to side as the water lapped against it. "I guess you're right. But before we go . . ." She pulled Jean-Claude toward her for one more lingering kiss, and then one more after that.

They didn't stop until the first raindrops began to fall and the sky turned an ominous dark gray. Suddenly they were grabbing the blanket and everything on it, then dashing for the tiny sailboat, hoping that they would get back to the mainland before the worst of the storm hit.

The exhibit was everything Elizabeth had imagined. Large, dramatic oil paintings hung on the stark, white walls of the spacious gallery. Elegant men and women sipped champagne while studying the abstract figures that danced in floods of changing color on the canvases.

Perhaps what Elizabeth enjoyed most about the gathering was meeting Veronique, the daughter of the painter and a girl about Elizabeth's age. As Elizabeth, she was interested in writing, and after only a few minutes of conversation, it was clear that the two could be good friends. What was more, Veronique and Marc had taken to each other instantly as well. Elizabeth was delighted to see a real smile on Marc's face, the first since she had broken the news to him about Jessica.

Everything was falling into place. Elizabeth had found Marc and Veronique. Jessica had apparently met somebody special, Elizabeth surmised, judging from the quick disappearing act she had pulled on Marc. She was curious to know whom Jessica was seeing, but she was no longer so angry at her twin for sneaking behind Marc's back and hers. Everybody was happy now. That was the most important thing. Then there was René. . . .

Elizabeth frowned and then gave herself a scolding shake. The day was going too well for her to dwell on her frustration over his hostility. She turned her attention back to the colorful canvases.

"What do you think?" a deep voice behind her asked in English tinted by a French accent.

Elizabeth whirled around to see Veronique's

father, the painter, a middle-aged man with salt-and-pepper hair and a neatly trimmed beard and mustache. "You are studying the canvases as if you were an artist yourself."

Elizabeth blushed. "No, I'm not, but I love your paintings. The figures seem to—well, this may sound silly, but they seem to move with some kind of energy of their own."

"That doesn't sound at all silly. In fact, it is quite a compliment. Every artist dreams of creating work that has its own life."

Elizabeth was thrilled to talk with a real artist about his paintings. They chatted for several minutes. At the end of the conversation, Veronique's father extended his hand. "It has been a pleasure talking to you, Elizabeth. You are a very perceptive, intelligent young woman." Elizabeth blushed. What a day she was having!

She was still bubbling with excitement when she let herself into the Glizes' house later that afternoon. "Jess? Jessica?" She wanted to tell her twin about the exhibit. No response. "Hello? Is anyone home?" Her words echoed hollowly.

Elizabeth glanced at her watch. Five o'clock. That morning Jessica had told her she would be home by three-thirty. Typical. As the twins' father liked to say, "If I had a dollar for every time our Jess came home late, I'd be a rich man." Elizabeth had long guessed that when her parents wanted Jessica home by midnight, they set a curfew of eleven, giving her an hour to stretch her limit. Of course Jessica suspected this too, so she usually ignored her curfew altogether. She came home when she was ready to come home.

Elizabeth wasn't worried, although she did wonder once again whom her twin was with. She intended to find out as soon as Jessica got back. She would probably walk through the door at any moment.

But by six o'clock, Elizabeth was still alone, and she was beginning to get nervous. Even Jessica wasn't often over two hours late. The house seemed too big as Elizabeth wandered from room to room, peering out a window every few minutes to see if her sister was in sight. Rain streamed down the panes of glass. The wind howled viciously. No one came up the walk.

At six-thirty the telephone rang. Elizabeth ran for it, anticipating Jessica's voice on the other end. But Avery's deep lilt came over the line instead. "Elizabeth, I've been delayed here at my patient's. I should be home by eight, but I called to tell you kids not to wait for me for dinner. There's some chicken in the refrigerator that just needs to be reheated, and potatoes dauphinoise in a casserole. That can be warmed in the oven."

"Fine. I can fix the meal, but neither Jessica nor René is back yet."

"No? Well, René should be there shortly. He knows that dinner is at seven. But where's

Jessica? She's not planning to have dinner out, is she?"

"I don't know. She said she'd be home at three-thirty." Elizabeth heard the note of worry in her voice and made an attempt to control it. "But you know my sister," she added lightly. "She likes to take her time."

The joke fell flat. "Oh, my goodness." Avery sounded as concerned as Elizabeth. "Don't you think we ought to try to find her?"

"That's the trouble," Elizabeth explained tensely. "I don't have the slightest idea where she is."

"What about that boy she was spending time with, Marc? Can you call him?"

"She's not with him." Elizabeth didn't feel that this was the time to tell Avery about her sister and Marc. "But she'll show up. She always does," she added with bravado.

"Yes, I'm sure you're right," Avery said. "But please take my number and call me as soon as she arrives home, would you?"

"Of course." Elizabeth wrote down the number and said goodbye. Then she sat down to wait.

Fourteen

Elizabeth was panicky. It was seven o'clock. The wind was roaring now, and the trees tossed wildly. The windowpanes rattled with every fresh gust. She didn't have the vaguest notion about where to start looking for her twin. It wasn't the first time she had been worried about Jessica, but it was more scary in a foreign country, especially with a storm raging outside. Elizabeth felt totally, hopelessly alone.

She jumped up and held her breath as she heard a key in the front door. But she let out a heavy sigh of disappointment when René strode in.

"You don't look so overjoyed to see me," he remarked.

"Oh, no, you don't understand, René," Elizabeth protested. "I thought maybe it was Jessica. She's not home yet, and I don't have any idea where she might be." Her words poured out, her voice rising in desperation.

"Did you try Jean-Claude?" René asked. His tone was offhanded, but Elizabeth could feel his gaze on her, as if he was studying her for a reaction.

But she didn't understand. "Jean-Claude?" she asked, her brow furrowed.

"Don't tell me you're surprised. You stole her friend; she stole yours. An eye for an eye, that sort of thing. My friends saw Jessica and Jean-Claude together and told me."

Elizabeth didn't bother to reply to René's provocative comment. She was frantically trying to digest what he had just revealed about her twin and Jean-Claude. She remembered how interested Jessica had been when she'd told her about him. Perhaps too interested. Her head spun. What had Jessica engineered this time?

"You have nothing to say about that?" René broke into her thoughts. "But perhaps you knew already," he mused aloud. "Yes, now I see. You two arranged this whole thing. You decided to swap identities to get a laugh at the expense of Marc and Jean-Claude." He scowled. "God, don't you have any scruples?"

"René, what are you talking about?" Elizabeth spoke distractedly, still puzzling about how

Jessica had gotten together with Jean-Claude. "There wasn't any identity switching. Marc knows I'm Elizabeth and Jean-Claude—" She broke off in midsentence as the truth dawned on her.

"Jean-Claude thinks Jessica is you," René finished. "So much for your American sense of loyalty." He crossed his arms over his chest.

Now it made sense. No wonder Jean-Claude hadn't called her back. As far as he knew, they hadn't missed their date after all. While she had been stuck on the bus after taking the medicine to Avery, Jessica must have been at the house to stand in for her. Elizabeth felt anger growing within her. It wasn't the first time Jessica had pretended to be her. Of all the nasty, low-down tricks for her twin to pull. When Jessica got back, Elizabeth was going to sit her down and talk to her. But when was she going to get back?

Suddenly Elizabeth's fears about her sister rushed over her again, mingling with her anger. A bolt of lightning illuminated the sky outside. That did it! Angry or not, Elizabeth had to find Jessica. What if she was in trouble?

She rushed to the telephone and dialed the countess's number. It rang several times. *Come on, somebody be home,* Elizabeth pleaded silently. Finally the phone was picked up. Elizabeth instantly recognized the countess's voice.

"Hello, Countess. This is Elizabeth Wakefield."

"Elizabeth. What a relief. Are you and Jean-Claude all right? I was so worried."

"Countess, there's been, ah, a little, well, you might call it a mix-up." Elizabeth stumbled over her words. How did her sister get her into these situations? "Jean-Claude's not with me," she continued, "but I thought you might be able to tell me where he is."

"He went out to Ile Sainte-Marguerite," the countess said. "With you, I thought. He took his little sailboat."

Elizabeth glanced out the window at the wild winds and rain. A small boat was no match for this weather. "Oh, Countess, I've got to look for them—I mean, him. Do you know where he would have sailed from?"

"Probably from the beach near the Pointe de la Croisette. That's the mainland beach nearest to the island. I was about to have my chauffeur drive me over there."

"I'll go instead," Elizabeth volunteered. "I can't stand to sit here worrying for another second. If I find Jean-Claude, I'll tell him you're wondering where he is."

She said goodbye and rushed into the living room. "René, I need your help." She got straight to the point; there wasn't a second to waste. "Jessica and Jean-Claude may be in trouble. I've got to get to the beach off the Pointe de la Croisette. I know how you feel about Jess and me, but it's an emergency. Can you give me a ride there?"

"You mean you're not mad at her?" René looked incredulous.

"There's no time to be mad. Jessica may need me."

René looked dubious.

"Look at it outside." Elizabeth's voice rose. She pointed toward one of the windows. "Jessica and Jean-Claude took a tiny sailboat over to Ile Sainte-Marguerite. What if they were on their way back when this storm started? The sea can be a pretty powerful enemy." She looked straight at René. "You of all people should know that," she said softly.

The color drained from René's face. "Yes, it can be," he whispered.

"Then I beg you to take me down there. Don't let the tragedy that happened to your friend happen again."

René nodded with conviction. "Get a raincoat and let's go," he said. Elizabeth raced to her room and returned a few moments later with a rain slicker.

But she froze when they got outside and René handed her a motorcycle helmet. "Oh, no. You don't have the car," she cried, the realization dawning on her. Avery had driven to work, leaving René his moped.

"This is going to have to do," René said. "We

don't have a choice." He threw his leg over the seat.

Elizabeth didn't move. Her cousin Rexy had been killed in a motorcycle crash, and Elizabeth herself had been in a near-fatal accident. It was a rule in the Wakefield family not to travel by motorcycle, a rule that even Jessica obeyed.

But how would Elizabeth feel if something happened to Jessica because she refused to get on René's moped? Lightning split the sky. Elizabeth had to get to her twin. She made a decision. She put on the helmet and got on the bike.

In no time they were on their way. But the tiny windshield René had attached to the cycle's front was almost useless in this kind of raging rain. The drops pelted them like pieces of flying glass as soon as they picked up speed, causing René to steer cautiously.

Elizabeth hung on behind him. Her slicker was almost useless in the wind. Her skirt was soaking wet. She imagined all the disasters that could be befalling her sister at that very moment.

"Oh, please hurry," she coaxed him.

"Do you know how dangerous it is to be on a moped in this weather? If I go any faster, we might be the ones who are in trouble."

Elizabeth swallowed hard. She didn't need to be reminded. All she could do was cross her fingers and pray that they wouldn't be too late.

*   *   *

Back in Sweet Valley, Steven Wakefield was in his car, also hoping he wouldn't be too late—too late to tell Cara how special she was to him and to ask her to forgive him. She had been polite but distant on the telephone when he had called to say he needed to talk to her. Not that Steven could blame her after the way he'd behaved. He was grateful that she had agreed to see him at all.

He made a right turn down Roundtree Road, following the familiar route to her apartment. He crossed the rickety bridge over the brook, where he and Cara liked to picnic. All the landmarks on the way to her apartment were still there; the drive was the same one he had made so many times before. Yet the sights he knew so well seemed strangely out of place, somehow unreal.

He had been feeling this way from the moment he had realized what an enormous mistake he'd made. It was as if his entire world had been altered over the past few days. In a way, it had been. He had learned something important about himself, about how easy it was for him to be ensnared by emotions he thought he'd controlled. He knew he would be more sensitive to his own weakness in the future. And he also knew that he would never again take Cara Walker for granted.

Steven's mind whirled with puzzling thoughts. How could he have let this whole crazy thing happen? How could he have surrendered to a fantasy?

It was hard to find answers. Steven steered his old yellow VW into the parking lot beside Cara's building. One thing he was sure of was that he couldn't begin to make peace with himself until he had made peace with Cara.

He took the elevator to the fourth floor and rang the Walkers' door bell. He waited nervously, listening for footsteps. The door opened, and Cara's brother Charlie stood grinning up at Steven.

"Steve! Boy, how are you doing?" he asked easily.

Steven gave Charlie a swat on the arm. "Hi, sport. Visiting for vacation?" Cara's parents were divorced, and Charlie lived with their father, though he spent some holidays from school with his sister and mother. "Good to see you," Steven told him.

Then he caught sight of Cara coming toward them, elegant in a simple, deep-red dress, her dark hair loose around her shoulders. "Sport, listen, we've still got an appointment to shoot some hoops soon, but right now I need to be alone with your sister, OK?"

Charlie rolled his eyes. "Sure, so you can do some serious kissing and stuff. B-o-r-i-n-g!" he exclaimed.

"Charlie!" Cara said sternly.

Charlie stood his ground and grinned mischievously, relishing the opportunity to make a pest of himself.

"If I give you a quarter, will you go play in traffic?" Steven quipped.

"Heavy traffic," Cara added.

"I guess I know when I'm not wanted." Charlie backed out of the room, his hands up in a gesture of mock surrender.

Cara and Steven laughed, but as soon as Charlie was gone, the light moment faded. Awkwardness filled the space between them like a concrete barrier. Steven shifted from one foot to the other, his hands opening and closing nervously.

"Why don't you come in?" Cara suggested, as timidly as if this were a first date. She ushered him into the living room. "We'll have some privacy here."

Steven sat on the couch next to Cara, but he couldn't get comfortable. He inched closer to her, crossed his ankles, and tried to look casual. It was no use.

"Hey, Cara, I guess I just have to come right out and say it. I've been acting like a big jerk. No. Worse. I've been insensitive and unfair and just plain dumb. I owe you a huge apology." The words tumbled out.

Cara listened quietly. "Steven, you hurt me very badly."

"I realize that, and I can't say I'm sorry enough times. Cara, I don't want to cause you any pain. Not now and not ever." He looked up at her, and their eyes met. "I love you."

191

"Steve, are you sure it's me you care for and not Tricia's memory? I know how special she was to you."

"You're special to me, too, Cara. You've got to believe that."

"But no one can take Tricia's place." Cara's voice was full of sadness and resignation.

"Perhaps not." Steven continued to hold Cara's brown-eyed gaze. "But that's because no person can ever replace another. Tricia was unique. That's one thing I've learned during all of this. There isn't anyone else like her. But, Cara, you're unique, too. That's what it is to be human. Every person is an individual, we're all different. It sounds trite, but it's true. You've tried to tell me that, haven't you?"

Cara nodded, swallowing hard.

"I won't ever make the mistake of confusing one person for another again, no matter how much they look alike on the outside." Steven shook his head. "Listen to me. I'm getting all philosophical. What I really mean is that you're you, and I love you for who you are, not for who you're not. I'll never do anything like this again."

"Steven, maybe you'd better take some more time to think about what you really want," Cara said softly.

Steven felt a spark of pain. "You don't want to take me back?" He had prepared himself for the worst, but that couldn't stop the ache growing inside him.

"I *do* want to be with you," Cara insisted. "But I think maybe you're not so sure it's what you want."

"Cara, you've got to believe me. I've never been so certain about anything. I need you."

"You do?" Cara sounded uncertain.

"I do."

Tentatively Steven put an arm around Cara's shoulder. She sat stiffly at first. He kissed her cheek. She leaned in toward him ever so slightly. "Cara, I've missed you," he whispered tenderly.

Cara's lower lip trembled. "Steve, I've missed you, too." A single tear rolled down her cheek.

Steven wiped it away. "Don't cry, Cara. Please don't cry. I'm so sorry. So very sorry." His own eyes were moist, and there was a tickle in his throat.

"Steve, you don't have to apologize again," Cara said, sniffling. "I'm just crying because I was so afraid I would never be able to hold you like this again." She put her arms around him and laid her head against his chest.

"Does that mean you forgive me?" Steven asked.

Cara nodded, turning her face up toward his. He traced the contours of her cheeks with his fingertip. Her skin was so soft and smooth. "Cara, it *is* you," he said. "You're the only one for me." And then their lips met in a long, sweet embrace. For Steven Wakefield, everything was as it should be again.

On the beach at Cannes, however, everything was far from right. The winds whipped the sea into a frenzy. The normally calm water was angrily alive with waves and whitecaps. Pouring rain had long since drenched Elizabeth's clothing, but she was barely aware of it.

All her attention was focused on the little boat fighting its way toward shore. It struggled against the current of swirling water, the sail coming about often, as it varied its angle of approach in the ever-changing wind. Elizabeth barely breathed as she followed its halting progress. After what seemed an eternity, the boat came close enough for her to make out two figures on it.

"I think it's them," she screamed to René, her voice snatched by the howling wind. "Jessica! Jean-Claude! Oh, my God!" With every passing moment, the water got rougher.

René stood as far back on the beach as he could, terror in his eyes as he faced his enemy, the sea. Elizabeth was desperate for a word of reassurance, some sign on his part that he believed the boat would make it safely to shore. But she knew that René was the last person to believe the wrath of the ocean could be beaten. His lips were pressed tightly together with fear, and Elizabeth realized that he was rooted to the spot, too petrified to move a muscle.

Finally the flailing sailboat came close enough for Elizabeth to see for certain that her twin and Jean-Claude were on it. They battled the sea, coming in ten yards only to be pushed back five. Jean-Claude tugged at the sail while Jessica wrestled with the rudder.

Elizabeth couldn't bear to watch them, but she couldn't take her eyes off them, either. When a powerful gust from exactly the right direction sent them gliding in toward shore, Elizabeth nearly sobbed with relief.

But her sense of relief almost instantly disappeared. A huge wave approached the boat, and Elizabeth watched in terror as it overtook them. Jean-Claude lost control of the sail, and the boat tipped over to one side. As it slipped into the water, the sail swung around, and the boom struck Jessica's head with the force of a club. Elizabeth saw her twin's body go limp.

Elizabeth's screams split the air.

Jean-Claude, too, slid into the sea, bobbing up and down and sputtering water as he reached out to grab the base of the boat. He caught onto it and immediately looked around for Jessica.

"Over there! On the other side of the boat!" Elizabeth shrieked at the top of her lungs. She could see her sister's immobile body.

"He can't hear you!" René yelled.

Elizabeth ripped off her rain slicker, flung off

her shoes, and raced to the sea. Diving in, she swam with every ounce of strength she possessed. As she reached her sister, she saw that Jean-Claude had already found her and was trying to grab hold of her. But the waves were high, and he kept losing his grasp.

Elizabeth pushed forward until she was next to them. Jessica's eyes were closed, and her wet face was deathly pale. Elizabeth reached over and gripped her sister in the over-the-chest carry she had learned in lifesaving at school the year before. She stroked toward land with her free arm, scissor kicking with her legs. Panting and swallowing mouthfuls of saltwater, she worked every muscle until it burned. The shore didn't seem to be getting any closer.

Jean-Claude tried to keep up with her, but Elizabeth sensed that his strength was giving out. Hers was, also. All her lifesaving maneuvers had been practiced in a swimming pool, never in a swirling, furious sea. Her heart pounded in panic. They weren't going to make it.

Suddenly there was somebody else at her side in the water, firmly taking hold of Jessica. "Cup your hand under Jean-Claude's chin and tow him along," he was yelling. It was René! Despite his fear of the ocean and his friend's drowning, he was coming to her aid! Elizabeth realized how much courage it must have taken for him to push aside the terror he had experienced and plunge into the raging sea. She said a silent prayer of thanks.

Somehow, working together, they managed to help Jean-Claude to the shallow water and drag Jessica up to shore. They laid her down out of the rain, on the sheltered porch of a nearby beach restaurant. Jessica's lips parted, and she let out a moan.

"She's beginning to come around," René said.

She opened her eyes and saw Jean-Claude, who was leaning over her. Exhausted and pale, he looked neither right nor left, but straight at Jessica. She smiled weakly at him. "Jean-Claude," she murmured.

"Elizabeth. Thank God!" His voice was flooded with relief as he gently took Jessica in his arms. They drank in each other's gaze, enveloped in a private world of love and tenderness.

Elizabeth—the real Elizabeth—was stunned to see such strong feelings pass between her sister and this boy. The light in Jessica's eyes as she looked up at Jean-Claude was new and rare. Was this the same girl who never stayed with any one boy long enough to lose her heart? The girl who played at relationships as if they were card games? But there was no mistaking the look on her sister's face. Jessica was in love.

And so was Jean-Claude. "Thank goodness you're all right," he whispered in Jessica's ear. Then glancing away for a moment now that he knew she was going to be fine, he twisted around to take his first good look at the two people who had come to his rescue. Elizabeth realized that in the frenzy of the accident, he hadn't been able to focus clearly on anything besides getting himself and Jessica to safety.

Now, as he spotted Elizabeth, his jaw dropped open in shock. "What?" He looked down at Jessica, then back at Elizabeth, who was standing with René. He did a double take.

Jessica, too, turned her head to look at her twin. Elizabeth caught her eye and saw her make a silent plea. It touched her. She hadn't forgotten that Jessica had tricked her in the most devious manner, but she was so happy her sister was alive that she was willing to forgive her almost anything.

Her eyes still holding her twin's, Elizabeth took a few steps toward Jean-Claude. Then she faced him directly. She held out her hand. "Hello," she said. "I'm Jessica, Elizabeth's sister."

Fifteen

"Can I offer you two a ride home?" Jean-Claude asked René and Elizabeth. "René, you can lock your moped up here and come back for it when the rain stops."

"Thanks, Jean-Claude, but it looks as if it's letting up. I'm so drenched anyway, I might as well ride it home now so I don't have to get it later. But by all means get these girls home immediately so they can change out of their wet clothes and my mother can take a look at her." He pointed at Jessica.

Elizabeth couldn't believe her ears. René was actually looking out for her and Jessica. Was he making a peace offering? "Thank you, René." She gave him a tentative smile.

René looked embarrassed. "Don't thank me. Thank Jean-Claude. He's the one who's driving you." He swung his leg over his bike. "Guess I'll see you back at the house," he added gruffly, but without the angry, hostile note in his voice that Elizabeth was so used to hearing.

"Yeah, see you there," Elizabeth said. "And, René, without you, we would all be—well, I hate to think about what could have happened. I can't tell you how grateful I am."

Jean-Claude added his heartfelt thanks, and even Jessica gave him a nod of appreciation.

"I did what I had to do," René said modestly, starting his moped and taking off.

Elizabeth watched him as he rode away. Something had happened between them out there in the foaming waves. They had joined forces, they had worked together, they had been a team. It wasn't as if they had suddenly become best friends, but it was a start.

"Liz, where's the purple shirt you brought with you?" asked Jessica. "It'll go great with these." She pulled on a pair of black stirrup pants that clung to her body.

"Don't you think you ought to take it easy after what you've just been through?" Elizabeth was sitting on the edge of her bed, watching Jessica dress.

"I *am* going to take it easy—with Jean-Claude.

And I don't want to make him wait all night, so can you hand over the shirt?" Jessica tapped her foot impatiently. Jean-Claude was sitting out front in his car, still wet, waiting for her.

Elizabeth crossed her arms. "I just can't believe that a half hour after René and I saved you from drowning, you're ready to go out to dinner."

"Look, I've thanked you a hundred and thirty-seven times for pulling me out of there, and I appreciate your concern, but I'm absolutely fine. You heard what Avery said. I just have a bump on my head. No dizziness, no headache. She said I was perfectly all right. And she should know, being a nurse and all. Besides, I have to eat anyway. Why not with Jean-Claude? Now the shirt, please."

Elizabeth sighed. "Oh, all right. Nothing I say is going to make any difference anyway." She dug the purple shirt out of her drawer and handed it to Jessica.

"Thanks." Jessica gave her a quick hug, then pulled the shirt over her head and surveyed herself in the mirror. She added a pair of dangling rhinestone earrings and the new shoes she had bought in Sweet Valley. Perfect.

"Well, see you, Liz." She headed for the door, but Elizabeth's voice stopped her.

"Hey, Jessica? Something just occurred to me."

"Yeah?" She turned around.

"When I was trying to find out where you and Jean-Claude were, I called the countess."

"So?" Jessica couldn't figure out what her twin was driving at.

"So I told her who was calling. She's going to think it's pretty strange when Jean-Claude says he was with Elizabeth during all of this."

Jessica groaned. "Oh, no. Why'd you have to go and say who you were?" Just when she had thought she was home free in this whole identity mess! "I mean you told Jean-Claude you were me. Why couldn't you have told the countess the same thing? I don't get it."

Elizabeth's brow creased. "Maybe you think fibbing to people is just a game, but for me it's most definitely not. I guess you can't understand how hard it was for me to lie to Jean-Claude about who I was back on the beach. I did it only because I could see how much you care about him."

"I do." Jessica softened. "And I know I probably don't deserve what you did for me."

"Probably not. But anyway, I didn't know what was happening between you and Jean-Claude when I talked to the countess, so why would I even think of telling her I was you?"

"Couldn't you guess that I was falling in love? Liz, why else would I sneak off with Jean-Claude the way I did? Is your opinion of me so bad that you think I'd do something like that just for the heck of it?" Jessica put on her best hurt expres-

202

sion. "I know I pulled kind of a, well, a rotten move on you, but it was for a really good reason. I *had* to do it. You've got to believe that."

"I think the bump on your head affected you, after all. How could I possibly think you were in love with Jean-Claude when I didn't know you were sneaking behind my back to see him? Jess, you should have told me how you felt about him right from the beginning."

Jessica toyed with a lock of hair, twisting it around her index finger. Elizabeth had been so grateful to see her safe, that Jessica thought she had gotten off without having to go into this. Now she could see she had been wrong. If only she had left the room a moment earlier, she wouldn't have had to discuss the whole situation.

"I thought about telling you," she replied lamely. "I wanted to."

Elizabeth looked at her steadily, saying nothing.

"But I just couldn't. Don't you see?" Jessica's voice rose to a wail. "What if you had made me tell Jean-Claude? Or what if you'd been so mad at me that you'd told him yourself? He might have decided I was too horrible to have anything to do with."

"So you'd rather have a relationship based on a lie. Is that it?"

"I'd rather have Jean-Claude than not have him," Jessica said with exasperation, "which means I'd better come up with some way to explain things to the countess, before the real story comes out." This was getting far too sticky for her. Why couldn't she and Jean-Claude simply enjoy each other without all the complications?

Elizabeth was no help. "I don't know what to tell you, Jessica."

"Liz, you're the writer. You think up stories all the time. Can't you think of one for me to tell the countess?" Jessica felt herself growing desperate. She couldn't blow things with Jean-Claude now. They had come through too much together.

"Sorry. The countess is one person you're going to have to tackle on your own," Elizabeth said.

Jessica opened her blue-green eyes wide, wordlessly pleading with her twin to help her out. It had worked on the beach. Maybe it would work again.

But Elizabeth stood her ground. "This part isn't my problem."

"But, Liz . . ."

"But, Jess. Don't you think I've done enough for you already? Think about it."

Jessica couldn't argue with her sister. Elizabeth would have had a perfect right to tell the whole world how she had been duped by her very own twin. Instead she had stood by her.

"You're right, Liz. You have done enough.

And don't worry about the countess. I'll figure out something to tell her."

"Of course you will. You always do, don't you?" Elizabeth shook her head, but it was obvious that she wasn't as upset anymore.

Jessica smiled. "Yup, I guess I do." She started to leave again but doubled back to throw her arms around her sister. "Liz, in case I haven't put it plainly enough, thanks for what you did for me today. Not just for fishing me out of the water, but for covering for me the way you did. I don't know what I would have done without you."

"Well, for starters, you wouldn't have met Jean-Claude at all," Elizabeth remarked teasingly. "Speaking of which, he's still waiting out there, and I'll bet he's good and ready to go home and change into some dry clothes."

Jessica needed no further coaxing. "Say no more," she told her twin. In no time flat she was racing out the front door and into Jean-Claude's damp but tender embrace.

A short while later, there was a light knock on Elizabeth's door. "Come on in," she called out.

The door swung open. It was René, his face pink from a hot shower, his wet hair combed back. He took a few uncertain steps into the room. Shyness colored his handsome features. "Hi," he said softly. "All changed and everything?" Then he gave a short laugh. "Kind of a dumb thing to say, huh? I can see for myself that you are."

Elizabeth felt a bit hesitant herself. "Yes, it's good to get into something dry and warm. Neither of us was exactly dressed for a swim," she joked nervously. After what had taken place down at the beach, Elizabeth no longer knew what to expect from René, or how to act toward him.

René stood awkwardly by the door, his hands stiffly at his sides.

"Oh, um, would you like to come in and sit down?" Elizabeth offered.

"Thanks." René crossed the room and lowered himself into the wooden chair in the far corner.

Then there was a long silence, broken only by the chirping of crickets outside and the rustling of the wind, quieting now, through the trees. Elizabeth looked at René, and he raised his eyes to meet her glance. Suddenly they both began to speak at once.

The ice was shattered, and they both laughed. "You first," Elizabeth said.

"No, you first. You're the guest."

"All right," Elizabeth agreed, composing her thoughts. "I'm glad you came in here. There's something I want to tell you." She sat down on the edge of her bed and faced René. "I know how tough it was for you to do what you did back at the beach. I mean because of your friend and all." She touched on the subject gingerly, remembering what had happened the first time she had mentioned the drowning.

René nodded. Elizabeth continued. "It was awfully brave of you, and I thank you deeply. I don't think I would have had the strength to help Jessica and Jean-Claude by myself." She swallowed hard, squeezing her eyes closed against the gruesome images of what might have been if she had had to fight the sea alone.

"I didn't have any choice," René said. "It was like seeing what happened to Antoine all over again. That was my friend's name. Antoine." A faraway look stole into René's deep-set green eyes.

Elizabeth waited patiently, respecting René's memories. He focused on her again, then spoke softly. "I couldn't let the same thing happen twice. I was petrified, but I had to make up for failing with Antoine."

"Failing? From what I've heard, you did everything possible to save your friend," Elizabeth said. "What happened wasn't your fault."

"People have been telling me the same thing ever since that day. In my head I realized it was true, but believing it in here was a different story." René pointed toward his chest. "I wanted a second chance, but of course it could never come. Today I finally recognized that I have to put the past behind me. My ability to care for and to help other people, didn't die with Antoine. Today you and I saved the lives of two people." There was a note of pride and thankfulness in René's voice. "It was different this time."

"Thank goodness," Elizabeth said. "But, René, there's one thing that's exactly the same. You did everything in your power both times. You have to stop blaming yourself for what happened to your friend."

"I think maybe now I can," René replied. "In a funny way, I have you and Jessica to thank for that, don't I?"

"And we have *you* to thank for Jessica's life. I can't say it enough. And one more thing." Elizabeth looked into his green eyes. "I'm very sorry if I've lost my temper with you."

"You had every reason to," René said. "I've behaved horribly. I saw what you did for your sister. I was wrong about you. I saw your devotion to her and how willing you were to overlook how she had deceived you. I owe you an apology, Elizabeth."

"I accept it," Elizabeth said, "and I also think I understand what you were feeling about Jessica and me. I know we must have been constant reminders of your father."

René nodded. "I guess I wasn't fooling anyone. But there's more to it than just that. I think I owe it to you to tell you." He took a deep breath. "You know, I decided right from the start that you were somebody to dislike, even before you

208

got here. But when you got off the plane you were so—well, so pretty. And you seemed really nice." René blushed and paused for a moment.

"There was something about you," he continued with embarrassment. "This is hard to say. I felt as if I could—you know, really like you. So I had to fight you extra hard. I couldn't let my defenses down. Not around someone I associated with my father. It was so much easier to be angry and hateful. I learned that when my father left. He didn't even say goodbye to me. The way one got hurt was by being too soft. At least that's what I thought until now. I guess I've been wrong about a lot of things. . . ."

"Even Americans?"

"Maybe." He smiled broadly.

Elizabeth felt a new sense of admiration for René. It had taken tremendous courage for him to admit his mistakes, and even more to expose his feelings for her. She returned his smile. "If you really are ready to give us Americans a chance, I have a letter addressed to you in my top drawer that I couldn't bring myself to throw out."

René paled, and for a moment Elizabeth was afraid she had gone too far. Then the smile returned to his face. "I'll tell you what. I'll read the letter if you promise to spend the day with me tomorrow. I want to start making up for the past few days."

"Well, I'm meeting Veronique Gallivère for breakfast. Do you know her?"

"I think so. Joseph Gallivère's daughter?"

Elizabeth nodded. "I met her at the opening of his show. She's really nice. I won't be able to do anything with you until the afternoon. Is that all right?"

"That's fine. Perhaps we can go to the beach," René suggested.

"The beach?" Elizabeth was surprised.

"Yes." René grinned. "It's been an awfully long time since I've gone for a nice, relaxing swim!"

"Good for you, René! I'd love to share that with you."

"And dinner afterward? That's part of the deal."

"You've got yourself a date," Elizabeth said. "By the way," she added shyly, "you made a confession to me, so it's only fair that I make one to you. When I first got here, I was sort of hoping we could be, ah, good friends," She remembered studying his picture on the airplane.

René's handsome face glowed. "I don't think it's too late."

Sixteen

"Liz, wake up! Come on, I have to tell you something!"

Elizabeth felt herself being jostled. Her lids heavy with sleep, she tried to open her eyes. "Wha—? What time is it? Jessica?"

"Yeah, it's me. Liz, are you awake?"

Elizabeth yawned and sat up in bed. "I am now," she replied groggily. "What do you want? It's the middle of the night."

"I know, but I just got home from my date with Jean-Claude, and I had to tell you. . . ." With an exuberant bounce, Jessica sat down on the edge of Elizabeth's bed.

"Tell me what?" Elizabeth asked, half of her still in dreamland.

"I came clean with Jean-Claude! I told him the truth, and he still loves me! Liz, isn't it fantastic?"

"Mmm. Fantastic," Elizabeth echoed, Jessica's image still blurry.

"Don't be too enthusiastic or anything," Jessica said wryly. "It's only the best thing that's happened to me in ages."

"Come on, Jess. I think it's wonderful news, and I'm really proud of you, but you can't expect me to jump up and down when I'm not even awake."

"Can't you get awake, Liz? This is important!"

"I know. It must have been awfully hard to tell Jean-Claude." Elizabeth stifled another yawn. "And it's great that you did, but can't we talk about this in the morning?" She lay back down and buried her head in her pillow.

"Look, you can go back to sleep in a second. I just want to tell you one more thing. Jean-Claude says he's sorry he stood you up that day. I told him you'd understand."

"I'm glad you took the liberty," Elizabeth said, with a touch of sarcasm.

If Jessica heard it, she gave no sign. "Oh, one more thing. The countess sends her best. She's a pretty neat old lady, after all. I thought she wouldn't want Jean-Claude ever to see me again after he told her what I'd done, but she was more intrigued than anything else. She said she couldn't quite figure out how I'd pulled it off."

"Did you explain that you've had years of experience?" Elizabeth asked.

"Oh, give me a break, Liz. I told Jean-Claude the truth in the end. Isn't that what you wanted?"

"Yeah, but I would rather have heard about it in the morning."

The corners of Jessica's mouth turned down in her most convincing pout. "I thought you'd want to know right away. I thought you cared what happened between Jean-Claude and me."

"I do care. I think I proved that this afternoon, didn't I?"

"Not this conversation again." Jessica rolled her eyes. "How'd we get on this? I thought we were talking about the countess. She said she'd like to see you, the real Elizabeth."

"I'd like to see her, too." Elizabeth pushed her pillow aside. She was beginning to wake up, even though she didn't want to.

"Jean-Claude invited me over tomorrow," Jessica said. "You can come by with me to visit his grandmother, if you feel like it."

"I can't. I'm meeting Veronique in the morning and I have plans in the afternoon."

"Veronique? Who's she?" Jessica demanded.

"Oh, that's right. With everything that's happened, I didn't get to tell you about my day," Elizabeth said. So much had occurred since the art exhibit, it was hard to believe it had been just

213

this past afternoon. "Veronique's a girl I met at this art opening Marc took me to."

"Marc!" screeched Jessica. "My Marc?"

Elizabeth was wide awake now. "You never wanted him to be your Marc for a second! And he finally got the hint. I have a feeling he's going to be Veronique's Marc pretty soon."

"Her again? Who is this girl? And, Liz, would you mind telling me how on earth you wound up going to an art opening with Marc? I don't get it." There was a note of annoyance in Jessica's voice.

"Jess, it all started when Marc came around here looking for you." Elizabeth patiently related the conversation and then told her sister all about the art exhibit.

"I see," Jessica said. "While I was feeling horribly guilty about sneaking off with Jean-Claude, you were busy making all kinds of new friends, and now you'd rather be with them than with me."

"Now, wait a minute." Elizabeth didn't intend to let herself be ensnared in Jessica's trap. "To begin with, you didn't feel guilty enough to stop seeing Jean-Claude or to tell me what was going on. And second, you should be happy for me that I've made some friends here. Besides, all I arranged with Veronique was a date for breakfast. That's not such a huge deal, is it?"

"Oh, I guess not. Besides, I don't plan on getting up before noon tomorrow anyway. You can come over to the de Willenichs' with me later in the afternoon."

Elizabeth wasn't sure Jessica was going to like what she had to tell her next. "I'm going to have to see the countess some other time. I'm spending the afternoon with René," she said quietly.

"Elizabeth Wakefield! I don't believe it! Wow, you've been holding out on telling me all kinds of things!"

"I haven't held out on anything, Jessica. All this stuff just happened today," Elizabeth protested.

"Why René, of all people?" Jessica made a face.

"After you left tonight, he came in to tell me he'd been wrong about me. We talked."

"But he's been such a pain."

"He saved your life."

"Yeah . . ."

"Jess, I was wrong about him, too. He's a nice guy. I like him."

Jessica was quiet for a moment. Her expression softened. "Liz, I just want you to be happy."

Elizabeth nodded, brushing a strand of flaxen hair away from her face. She knew her twin meant what she said. "I think I *will* be happy spending some time with René."

Suddenly Jessica broke into a grin. "I knew it!" she announced triumphantly. "I knew from the second I saw you looking at his picture on the plane that you and René were going to be—"

"Whoa! All I said was that I was spending the afternoon with René. As friends."

Jessica tossed Elizabeth a sly glance.

"Why are you looking at me like that?" Elizabeth asked, knowing full well what her sister meant. "We're going to get to know each other a little better, that's all."

"Sure, Liz." Jessica laughed.

"Jess, we're only going to be here for a few days. Then we'll be on our way back to Sweet Valley."

"That's exactly it," Jessica said. "A lot can happen between now and then! You'll see, Liz."

"I guess I will," Elizabeth answered. She had a feeling that these were going to be days that she wasn't likely to forget.

☐	24994	**RUNAWAY #21**	**$2.50**
☐	25133	**TOO MUCH IN LOVE #22**	**$2.50**
☐	25176	**SAY GOODBYE #23**	**$2.50**
☐	25243	**MEMORIES #24**	**$2.50**
☐	25299	**NOWHERE TO RUN #25**	**$2.50**
☐	25430	**HOSTAGE! #26**	**$2.50**
☐	25471	**LOVESTRUCK #27**	**$2.50**

EXCITING NEWS FOR ROMANCE READERS

Love Letters—the all new, hot-off-the-press Romance Newsletter. Now you can be the first to know:

What's Coming Up:
* Exciting offers
* New romance series on the way

What's Going Down:
* The latest gossip about the SWEET VALLEY HIGH gang
* Who's in love . . . and who's not

Who's Who:
* The real life stories about SWEET DREAMS cover girls
* The true facts about SWEET DREAMS authors

Who's New:
* Meet Kelly Blake
* Find out who's a *Winner* And much, much more!

Fill out this coupon, mail it in, and this spring your free copy of *Love Letters* is on its way to you. *Love Letters*—you're going to love it.

Please send me my free copy of Love Letters

Name _____ Age _____

Address _____

City _____ State _____ Zip _____

To: BANTAM BOOKS
Dept. KR
666 Fifth Avenue
New York, NY 10103

SD6—2/86